Tartarin On The Alps

Alphonse Daudet

Translator: Katharine Prescott Wormeley

Contents

TARTARIN ON THE ALPS

BY

Alphonse Daudet

Translator: Katharine Prescott Wormeley

TARTARIN ON THE ALPS.
By Alphonse Daudet

TARTARIN ON THE ALPS.
I.

Apparition on the Rigi-Kulm. Who is it? What was said around a table of six hundred covers. Rice and Prunes, An improvised ball. The Unknown signs his name on the hotel register, P. C. A.

On the 10th of August, 1880, at that fabled hour of the setting sun so vaunted by the guide-books Joanne and Baedeker, an hermetic yellow fog, complicated with a flurry of snow in white spirals, enveloped the summit of the Rigi (*Regina montium*) and its gigantic hotel, extraordinary to behold on the arid waste of those heights,--that Rigi-Kulm, glassed-in like a conservatory, massive as a citadel, where alight for a night and a day a flock of tourists, worshippers of the sun.

While awaiting the second dinner-gong, the transient inmates of the vast and gorgeous caravansary, half frozen in their chambers above, or gasping on the divans of the reading-rooms in the damp heat of lighted furnaces, were gazing, in default of the promised splendours, at the whirling white atoms and the lighting of the great lamps on the portico, the double glasses of which were creaking in the wind.

To climb so high, to come from all four corners of the earth to see that... Oh, Baedeker!..

Suddenly, something emerged from the fog and advanced toward the hotel with a rattling of metal, an exaggeration of motions, caused by strange accessories.

At a distance of twenty feet through the fog the torpid tourists, their noses against the panes, the **misses** with curious little heads trimmed like those of boys, took this apparition for a cow, and then for a tinker bearing his utensils.

Ten feet nearer the apparition changed again, showing a crossbow on the shoulder, and the visored cap of an archer of the middle ages, with the visor lowered, an object even more unlikely to meet with on these heights than a strayed cow or an ambulating tinker.

On the portico the archer was no longer anything but a fat, squat, broad-backed man, who stopped to get breath and to shake the snow from his leggings, made like his cap of yellow cloth, and from his knitted comforter, which allowed scarcely more of his face to be seen than a few tufts of grizzling beard and a pair of enormous green spectacles made as convex as the glass of a stereoscope. An alpenstock, knapsack, coil of rope worn in saltire, crampons and iron hooks hanging to the belt of an English blouse with broad pleats, completed the accoutrement of this perfect Alpinist.

On the desolate summits of Mont Blanc or the Finsteraarhorn this clambering apparel would have seemed very natural, but on the Rigi-Kulm ten feet from a railway track!--

The Alpinist, it is true, came from the side opposite to the station, and the state of his leggings testified to a long march through snow and mud.

For a moment he gazed at the hotel and its surrounding buildings, seemingly stupefied at finding, two thousand and more yards above the sea, a building of such importance, glazed galleries, colonnades, seven storeys of windows, and a broad portico stretching away between two rows of globe-lamps which gave to this mountain-summit the aspect of the Place de l'Opera of a winter's evening.

But, surprised as he may have been, the people in the hotel were more surprised still, and when he entered the immense antechamber an inquisitive hustling took place in the doorways of all the salons: gentlemen armed with billiard-cues, others with open newspapers, ladies still holding their book or their work pressed forward, while in the background, on the landing of the staircase, heads leaned over the baluster and between the chains of the lift.

The man said aloud, in a powerful deep bass voice, the chest voice of the South, resounding like cymbals:--

"***Coquin de bon sort!*** what an atmosphere!"

Then he stopped short, to take off his cap and his spectacles.

He was suffocating.

The dazzle of the lights, the heat of the gas and furnace, in contrast with the cold darkness without, and this sumptuous display, these lofty ceilings, these porters bedizened with ***Regina Montium*** in letters of gold on their naval caps, the white cravats of the waiters and the battalion of Swiss girls in their native costumes coming forward at sound of the gong, all these things bewildered him for a second--but only one.

He felt himself looked at and instantly recovered his self-possession, like a comedian facing a full house.

"Monsieur desires..?"

This was the manager of the hotel, making the inquiry with the tips of his teeth, a very dashing manager, striped jacket, silken whiskers, the head of a lady's dressmaker.

The Alpinist, not disturbed, asked for a room, "A good little room, ***au mouain?***" perfectly at ease with that majestic manager, as if with a former schoolmate.

But he came near being angry when a Bernese servant-girl, advancing, candle in hand, and stiff in her gilt stomacher and puffed muslin sleeves, inquired if Monsieur would be pleased to take the lift. The proposal to commit a crime would not have made him more indignant.

"A lift! he!.. for him!.." And his cry, his gesture, set all his metals rattling.

Quickly appeased, however, he said to the maiden, in an amiable tone: "***Pedibusse cum jambisse***, my pretty little cat..." And he went up behind her, his broad back filling the stairway, parting the persons he met on his way, while throughout the hotel the clamorous questions ran: "Who is he? What's this?" muttered in the divers languages of all four quarters of the globe. Then the second dinner-gong sounded, and nobody thought any longer of this extraordinary personage.

A sight to behold, that dining-room of the Rigi-Kulm.

Six hundred covers around an immense horseshoe table, where tall, shallow dishes of rice and of prunes, alternating in long files with green plants, reflected in their dark or transparent sauces the flame of the candles in the chandeliers and the gilding of the panelled ceiling.

As in all Swiss **tables d'hote**, rice and prunes divided the dinner into two rival factions, and merely by the looks of hatred or of hankering cast upon those dishes it was easy to tell to which party the guests belonged. The Rices were known by their anaemic pallor, the Prunes by their congested skins.

That evening the latter were the most numerous, counting among them several important personalities, European celebrities, such as the great historian Astier-Rehu, of the French Academy, Baron von Stolz, an old Austro-Hungarian diplomat, Lord Chipendale (?), a member of the Jockey-Club and his niece (h'm, h'm!), the illustrious doctor-professor Schwanthaler, from the University of Bonn, a Peruvian general with eight young daughters.

To these the Rices could only oppose as a picket-guard a Belgian senator and his family, Mme. Schwanthaler, the professor's wife, and an Italian tenor, returning from Russia, who displayed his cuffs, with buttons as big as saucers, upon the tablecloth.

It was these opposing currents which no doubt caused the stiffness and embarrassment of the company. How else explain the silence of six hundred half-frozen, scowling, distrustful persons, and the sovereign contempt they appeared to affect for one another? A superficial observer might perhaps have attributed this stiffness to stupid Anglo-Saxon haughtiness which, nowadays, gives the tone in all countries to the travelling world.

No! no! Beings with human faces are not born to hate one another thus at first sight, to despise each other with their very noses, lips, and eyes for lack of a previous introduction. There must be another cause.

Rice and Prunes, I tell you. There you have the explanation of the gloomy silence weighing upon this dinner at the Rigi-Kulm, which, considering the number and international variety of the guests, ought to have been lively, tumultuous, such as we imagine the repasts at the foot of the Tower of Babel to have been.

The Alpinist entered the room, a little overcome by this refectory of monks, apparently doing penance beneath the glare of chandeliers; he coughed noisily without any one taking notice of him, and seated himself in his place of last-comer at the end of the room. Divested of his accoutrements, he was now a tourist like any other, but of aspect more amiable, bald, barrel-bellied, his beard pointed and bunchy, his nose majestic, his eyebrows thick and ferocious, overhanging the glance of a downright good fellow.

Rice or Prunes? No one knew as yet.

Hardly was he installed before he became uneasy, and leaving his place with an alarming bound: "Ouf! what a draught!" he said aloud, as he sprang to an empty chair with its back laid over on the table.

He was stopped by the Swiss maid on duty--from the canton of Uri, that one-- silver chains and white muslin chemisette.

"Monsieur, this place is engaged..."

Then a young lady, seated next to the chair, of whom the Alpinist could see only her blond hair rising from the whiteness of virgin snows, said, without turning round, and with a foreign accent:

"That place is free; my brother is ill, and will not be down."

"Ill?.." said the Alpinist, seating himself, with an anxious, almost affectionate manner... "Ill? Not dangerously, *au moins*."

He said *au mouain*, and the word recurred in all his remarks, with other vocable parasites, such as *he, que, tey zou, ve, vai, et autrement, differemment*, etc., still further emphasized by a Southern accent, displeasing, apparently, to the young lady, for she answered with a glacial glance of a black blue, the blue of an abyss.

His neighbour on the right had nothing encouraging about him either; this was the Italian tenor, a gay bird with a low forehead, oily pupils, and the moustache of a matador, which he twirled with nervous fingers at being thus separated from his pretty neighbour. But the good Alpinist had a habit of talking as he ate; it was necessary for his health.

" *Ve!* the pretty buttons..." he said to himself, aloud, eying the cuffs of his neighbour. "Notes of music, inlaid in jasper--why, the effect is *charmain!*.."

His metallic voice rang on the silence, but found no echo.

"Surely monsieur is a singer, *que?*"

"*Non capisco*," growled the Italian into his moustache.

For a moment the man resigned himself to devour without uttering a word, but the morsels choked him. At last, as his opposite neighbour, the Austro-Hungarian diplomat, endeavoured to reach the mustard-pot with the tips of his shaky old fingers, covered with mittens, he passed it to him obligingly. "Happy to serve you, Monsieur le baron," for he had heard some one call him so.

Unfortunately, poor M. de Stoltz, in spite of his shrewd and knowing air contracted in diplomatic juggling, had now lost both words and ideas, and was travelling among the mountains for the special purpose of recovering them. He opened his eyes wide upon that unknown face, and shut them again without a word. It would have taken ten old diplomats of his present intellectual force to have constructed in common a formula of thanks.

At this fresh failure the Alpinist made a terrible grimace, and the abrupt manner in which he seized the bottle standing near him might have made one fear he was about to cleave the already cracked head of the diplomatist Not so! It was only to offer wine to his pretty neighbour, who did not hear him, being absorbed by a semi-whispered conversation in a soft and lively foreign warble with two young men seated next to her. She bent to them, and grew animated. Little frizzles of hair were seen shining in the light against a dainty, transparent, rosy ear... Polish, Russian, Norwegian?.. from the North certainly; and a pretty song of those distant lands coming to his lips, the man of the South began tranquilly to hum:--

O coumtesso gento,
Estelo dou Nord,
Que la neu argento,
Qu' Amour friso en or. {*}

* O pretty countess,
Light of the North,
Which the snow silvers,
And Love curls in gold.

(Frederic Mistral.)

The whole table turned round; they thought him mad. He coloured, subsided into his plate, and did not issue again except to repulse vehemently one of the sacred compote-dishes that was handed to him.

"Prunes! again!.. Never in my life!"

This was too much.

A grating of chairs was heard. The academician, Lord Chipendale (?), the Bonn professor, and other notabilities rose, and left the room as if protesting.

The Rices followed almost immediately, on see-tog the second compote-dish rejected as violently as the first.

Neither Rice nor Prunes!.. then what?..

All withdrew; and it was truly glacial, that silent defile of scornful noses and mouths with their corners disdainfully turned down at the luckless man, who was left alone in the vast gorgeous dining-room, engaged in sopping his bread in his wine after the fashion of his country, crushed beneath the weight of universal disdain.

My friends, let us never despise any one. Contempt is the resource of parvenus, prigs, ugly folk, and fools; it is the mask behind which nonentity shelters itself, and sometimes blackguardism; it dispenses with mind, judgment, and good-will. All humpbacked persons are contemptuous; all crooked noses wrinkle with disdain when they see a straight one.

He knew that, this worthy Alpinist. Having passed, by several years, his "fortieth," that landing on the fourth storey where man discovers and picks up the magic key which opens life to its recesses, and reveals its monotonous and deceptive labyrinth; conscious, moreover, of his value, of the importance of his mission, and of the great name he bore, he cared nothing for the opinion of such persons as these. He knew that he need only name himself and cry out "'Tis I..." to change to grovelling respect those haughty lips; but he found his incognito amusing.

He suffered only at not being able to talk, to make a noise, unbosom himself, press hands, lean familiarly on shoulders, and call men by their Christian names. That is what oppressed him on the Rigi-Kulm.

Oh! above all, not being able to speak.

"I shall have dyspepsia as sure as fate," said the poor devil, wandering about the hotel and not knowing what to do with himself.

He entered a cafe, vast and deserted as a church on a week day, called the waiter, "My good friend," and ordered "a mocha without sugar, *que'*." And as the waiter did not ask, "Why no sugar?" the Alpinist added quickly, "'Tis a habit I acquired in Africa, at the period of my great hunts."

He was about to recount them, but the waiter had fled on his phantom slippers to Lord Chipendale, stranded, full length, upon a sofa and crying, in mournful tones: "Tchempegne!.. tchempegne!.." The cork flew with its silly noise, and nothing more was heard save the gusts of wind in the monumental chimney and the hissing click of the snow against the panes.

Very dismal too was the reading-room; all the journals in hand, hundreds of heads bent down around the long green tables beneath the reflectors. From time to time a yawn, a cough, the rustle of a turned leaf; and soaring high above the calm of this hall of study, erect and motionless, their backs to the stove, both solemn and both smelling equally musty, were the two pontiffs of official history, Astier-Rehu and Schwanthaler, whom a singular fatality had brought face to face on the summit of the Rigi, after thirty years of insults and of rending each other to shreds in explanatory notes referring to "Schwanthaler, jackass," "*vir ineptissimus*, Astier-Rehu."

You can imagine the reception which the kindly Alpinist received on drawing up a chair for a bit of instructive conversation in that chimney corner. From the height of these two caryatides there fell upon him suddenly one of those currents of air of which he was so afraid. He rose, paced the hall, as much to warm himself as to recover self-confidence, and opened the bookcase. A few English novels lay scattered about in company with several heavy Bibles and tattered volumes of the Alpine Club. He took up one of the latter, and carried it off to read in bed, but was forced to leave it at the door, the rules not allowing the transference of the library to the chambers.

Then, still continuing to wander about, he opened the door of the billiard-room, where the Italian tenor, playing alone, was producing effects of torso and cuffs for the edification of their pretty neighbour, seated on a divan, between the two young men, to whom she was reading a letter. On the entrance of the Alpinist she stopped, and one of the young men rose, the taller, a sort of moujik, a dog-man, with hairy paws, and long, straight, shining black hair joining an unkempt beard. He made two steps in the direction of the new-comer, looked at him provocatively, and so fiercely that the worthy Alpinist, without demanding an explanation, made a prudent and judicious half-turn to the right.

"*Differemment*, they are not affable, these Northerners," he said aloud; and he shut the door noisily, to prove to that savage that he was not afraid of him.

The salon remained as a last refuge; he went there... ***Coquin de sort!***... The morgue, my good friends, the morgue of the Saint-Bernard where the monks expose the frozen bodies found beneath the snows in the various attitudes in which congealing death has stiffened them, can alone describe that salon of the Rigi-Kulm.

All those numbed, mute women, in groups upon the circular sofas, or isolated and fallen into chairs here and there; all those misses, motionless be-. neath the lamps on the round tables, still holding in their hands the book or the work they were employed on when the cold congealed them. Among them were the daughters of the general, eight little Peruvians with saffron skins, their features convulsed, the vivid ribbons on their gowns contrasting with the dead-leaf tones of English fashions; poor little *sunny-climes*, easy to imagine as laughing and frolicking beneath their cocoa-trees and now more distressing to behold than the rest in their glacial, mute condition. In the background, before the piano, was the death-mask of the old diplomat, his mittened hands resting inert upon the keyboard, the yellowing tones of which were reflected on his face.

Betrayed by his strength and his memory, lost in a polka of his own composition, beginning it again and again, unable to remember its conclusion, the unfortunate Stoltz had gone to sleep while playing, and with him all the ladies on the Rigi, nodding, as they slumbered, romantic curls, or those peculiar lace caps, in shape like the crust of a vol-au-vent, that English dames affect, and which seem to be part of the canf of travelling.

The entrance of the Alpinist did not awaken them, and he himself had dropped upon a divan, overcome by such icy discouragement, when the sound of vigorous, joyous chords burst from the vestibule; where three "musicos," harp, flute, and violin, ambulating minstrels with pitiful faces, and long overcoats flapping their legs, who infest the Swiss hostelries, had just arrived with their instruments.

At the very first notes our man sprang up as if galvanized.

"*Zou!* bravo!.. forward, music!"

And off he went, opening the great doors, feting the musicians, soaking them with champagne, drunk himself without drinking a drop, solely with the music which brought him back to life. He mimicked the piston, he mimicked the harp, he snapped his fingers over his head, and rolled his eyes and danced his steps, to the utter stupefaction of the tourists running in from all sides at the racket. Then suddenly, as the exhilarated musicos struck up a Strauss waltz with the fury of true tziganes, the Alpinist, perceiving in the doorway the wife of Professor Schwantha-ler, a rotund little Viennese with mischievous eyes, still youthful in spite of her powdered gray hair, he sprang up her, caught her by the waist, and whirled her into the room, crying put to the others; "Come on! come on! let us waltz!"

The impetus was given, the hotel thawed and twirled, carried off its centre. People danced in the vestibule, in the salon, round the long green table of the reading-room. 'Twas that devil of a man who set fire to ice. He, however, danced no more, being out of breath at the end of a couple of turns; but he guided his ball, urged the musicians, coupled the dancers, cast into the arms of the Bonn profes-sor an elderly Englishwoman; and into those of the austere Astier-Rehu the friski-est of the Peruvian damsels. Resistance was impossible. From that terrible Alpinist issued I know not what mysterious aura which lightened and buoyed up every one. And ***zou! zou! zou!*** No more contempt and disdain. Neither Rice nor Prunes, only waltzers. Presently the madness spread; it reached the upper storeys, and up through the well of the staircase could be seen to the sixth-floor landing the heavy and high-coloured skirts of the Swiss maids on duty, twirling with the stiffness of automatons before a musical chalet.

Ah! the wind may blow without and shake the lamp-posts, make the telegraph wires groan, and whirl the snow in spirals across that desolate summit Within all are warm, all are comforted, and remain so for that one night.

"***Differemment***, I must go to bed, myself," thought the worthy Alpinist, a pru-dent man, coming from a country where every one packs and unpacks himself rap-idly. Laughing in his grizzled beard, he slipped away, covertly escaping Madame Schwanthaler, who was seeking to hook him again ever since that initial waltz.

He took his key and his bedroom candle; then, on the first landing, he paused a moment to enjoy his work and to look at the mass of congealed ones whom he had forced to thaw and amuse themselves.

A Swiss maid approached him all breathless from the waltz, and said, present-ing a pen and the hotel register:--

"Might I venture to ask t***mossie*** to be so good as to sign his name?"

He hesitated a moment. Should he, or should he not preserve his incognito?

After all, what matter! Supposing that the news of his presence on the Rigi should reach ***down there***, no one would know what he had come to do in Switzerland. And besides, it would be so droll to see, to-morrow morning, the stupor of those "Inglichemans" when they should learn the truth... For that Swiss girl, of course, would not hold her tongue... What surprise, what excitement throughout the hotel!..

"Was it really he?.. he?.. himself?.." These reflections, rapid and vibrant, passed through his head like the notes of a violin in an orchestra. He took the pen, and with careless hand he signed, beneath Schwanthaler, Astier-Rehu, and other notabilities, the name that eclipsed them all, his name; then he went to his room, without so much as glancing round to see the effect, of which he was sure.

Behind him the Swiss maid looked at the name:

TARTARIN OF TARASCON,

beneath which was added:

P. C. A.

She read it, that Bernese girl, and was not the least dazzled. She did not know what P. C. A. signified, nor had she ever heard of "Dardarin."

Barbarian, *Vai!*

II.

Tarascon, five minutes' stop! The Club of the Alpines. Explanation of P. C. A. Rabbits of warren and cabbage rabbits. This is my last will and testament. The Sirop de cadavre. First ascension, Tartarin takes out his spectacles.

When that name "Tarascon" sounds trumpetlike along the track of the Paris-Lyons-Mediterranean, in the limpid, vibrant blue of a Provencal sky, inquisitive heads are visible at all the doors of the express train, and from carriage to carriage the travellers say to each other: "Ah! here is Tarascon!.. Now, for a look at Tarascon."

What they can see of it is, nevertheless, nothing more than a very ordinary, quiet, clean little town with towers, roofs, and a bridge across the Rhone. But the Tarasconese sun and its marvellous effects of mirage, so fruitful in surprises, inventions, delirious absurdities, this joyous little populace, not much larger than a chick-pea, which reflects and sums up in itself the instincts of the whole French South, lively, restless, gabbling, exaggerated, comical, impressionable--that is what the people on the express-train look out for as they pass, and it is that which has made the popularity of the place.

In memorable pages, which modesty prevents him from mentioning more explicitly, the historiographer of Tarascon essayed, once upon a time, to depict the happy days of the little town, leading its club life, singing its romantic songs (each his own) and, for want of real game, organizing curious cap-hunts. Then, war having come and the dark times, Tarascon became known by its heroic defence, its torpedoed esplanade, the club and the Cafe de la Comedie, both made impregnable; all the inhabitants enrolled in guerilla companies, their breasts braided with death's head and cross-bones, all beards grown, and such a display of battle-axes, boarding cutlasses, and American revolvers that the unfortunate inhabitants ended by frightening themselves and no longer daring to approach one another in the streets.

Many years have passed since the war, many a worthless almanac has been put in the fire, but Tarascon has never forgotten; and, renouncing the futile amusements of other days, it thinks of nothing now but how to make blood and muscle for the service of future revenge. Societies for pistol-shooting and gymnastics, costumed and equipped, all having band and banners; armouries, boxing-gloves, single-sticks, list-shoes; foot races and flat-hand fights between persons in the best society; these things have taken the place of the former cap-hunts and the platonic cynegetical discussions in the shop of the gunsmith Costecalde.

And finally the club, the old club itself, abjuring bouillotte and bezique, is now transformed into a "Club Alpin" under the patronage of the famous Alpine Club of London, which has borne even to India the fame of its climbers. With this difference, that the Tarasconese, instead of expatriating themselves on foreign summits, are content with those they have in hand, or rather underfoot, at the gates of their town.

"The Alps of Tarascon?" you ask. No; but the Alpines, that chain of mountainettes, redolent of thyme and lavender, not very dangerous, nor yet very high (five to six hundred feet above sea-level), which make an horizon of blue waves along the Provencal roads and are decorated by the local imagination with the fabulous and characteristic names of: Mount Terrible; The End of the World; The Peak of the Giants, etc.

'T is a pleasure to see, of a Sunday morning, the gaitered Tarasconese, pickaxe in hand, knapsack and tent on their backs, starting off, bugles in advance, for ascensions, of which the **Forum**, the local journal, gives full account with a descriptive luxury and wealth of epithets--abysses, gulfs, terrifying gorges--as if the said ascension were among the Himalayas. You can well believe that from this exercise the aborigines have acquired fresh strength and the "double muscles" heretofore reserved to the only Tartarin, the good, the brave, the heroic Tartarin.

If Tarascon epitomizes the South, Tartarin epitomizes Tarascon. He is not only the first citizen of the town, he is its soul, its genius, he has all its finest whimseys. We know his former exploits, his triumphs as a singer (oh! that duet of "Robert le Diable" in Bezuquet's pharmacy!), and the amazing odyssey of his lion-hunts, from which he returned with that splendid camel, the last in Algeria, since deceased, laden with honours and preserved in skeleton at the town museum among other Tarasconese curiosities.

Tartarin himself has not degenerated; teeth still good and eyes good, in spite of his fifties; still that amazing imagination which brings nearer and enlarges all objects with the power of a telescope. He remains the same man as he of whom the brave Commander Bravida used to say: "He's a **lapin**..."

Or, rather, **two lapins!** For in Tartarin, as in all the Tarasconese, there is a warren race and a cabbage race, very clearly accentuated: the roving rabbit of the warren, adventurous, headlong; and the cabbage-rabbit, homekeeping, coddling, nervously afraid of fatigue, of draughts, and of any and all accidents that may lead to death.

We know that this prudence did not prevent him from showing himself brave and even heroic on occasion; but it is permissible to ask what he was doing on the Rigi (**Regina Montium**) at his age, when he had so dearly bought the right to rest and comfort.

To that inquiry the infamous Costecalde can alone reply.

Costecalde, gunsmith by trade, represents a type that is rather rare in Tarascon. Envy, base, malignant envy, is visible in the wicked curve of his thin lips, and a species of yellow bile, proceeding from his liver in puffs, suffuses his broad, clean-shaven, regular face, with its surface dented as if by a hammer, like an ancient coin of Tiberius or Caracalla. Envy with him is a disease, which he makes no attempt to hide, and, with the fine Tarasconese temperament that overlays everything, he sometimes says in speaking of his infirmity: "You don't know how that hurts me..."

Naturally the curse of Costecalde is Tartarin. So much fame for a single man! He everywhere! always he! And slowly, subterraneously, like a worm within the gilded wood of an idol, he saps from below for the last twenty years that triumphant renown, and gnaws it, and hollows it. When, in the evening, at the club, Tartarin relates his encounters with lions and his wanderings in the great Sahara, Costecalde sits by with mute little laughs, and incredulous shakes of the head.

"But the skins, *au mouain*, Costecalde... those lions' skins he sent us, which are there, in the salon of the club?.."

"*Te! pardi*... Do you suppose there are no furriers in Algeria?.."

"But the marks of the balls, all round, in the heads?"

"*Et autremain*, did n't we ourselves in the days of the cap-hunts see ragged caps torn with bullets at the hatters' for sale to clumsy shots?"

No doubt the long established fame of Tartarin as a slayer of wild beasts resisted these attacks; but the Alpinist in himself was open to criticism, and Costecalde did not deprive himself of the opportunity, being furious that a man should be elected as president of the "Club of the Alpines" whom age had visibly overweighted and whose liking, acquired in Algeria, for Turkish slippers and flowing garments predisposed to laziness.

In fact, Tartarin seldom took part in the ascensions; he was satisfied to accompany them with votive wishes, and to read in full session, with rolling eyes, and intonations that turned the ladies pale, the tragic narratives of the expeditions.

Costecalde, on the contrary, wiry, vigorous "Cock-leg," as they called him, was always the foremost climber; he had done the Alpines, one by one, planting on their summits inaccessible the banner of the Club, *La Tarasque*, starred in silver. Nevertheless, he was only vice-president, V. P. C. A. But he manipulated the place so well that evidently, at the coming elections, Tartarin would be made to skip.

Warned by his faithfuls--Bezuquet the apothecary, Excourbanies, the brave Commander Bravida--the hero was at first possessed by black disgust, by that indignant rancour which ingratitude and injustice arouse in the noblest soul. He wanted to quit everything, to expatriate himself, to cross the bridge and go and live in Beaucaire, among the Volsci; after that, he grew calmer.

To quit his little house, his garden, his beloved habits, to renounce his chair as president of the Club of the Alpines, founded by himself, to resign that majestic P. C. A. which adorned and distinguished his cards, his letter-paper, and even the lining of his hat! Not possible, *ve!* Suddenly there came into his head an electrifying idea...

In a word, the exploits of Costecalde were limited to excursions among the Alpines. Why should not Tartarin, during the three months that still intervened before the elections, why should he not attempt some grandiose adventure? plant, for instance, the standard of the Club on the highest peak of Europe, the Jungfrau or the Mont Blanc?

What triumph on his return! what a slap in the face to Costecalde when the *Forum* should publish an account of the ascension! Who would dare to dispute his presidency after that?

Immediately he set to work; sent secretly to Paris for quantities of works on Alpine adventure: Whymper's "Scrambles," Tyndall's "Glaciers," the "Mont-Blanc" of Stephen d'Arve, reports of the Alpine Club, English and Swiss; cramming his head with a mass of mountaineering terms--chimneys, couloirs, moulins, neves, seracs, moraines, rotures--without knowing very well what they meant.

At night, his dreams were fearful with interminable slides and sudden falls into bottomless crevasses. Avalanches rolled him down, icy aretes caught his body on the descent; and long after his waking and the chocolate he always took in bed, the agony and the oppression of that nightmare clung to him. But all this did not hinder him, once afoot, from devoting his whole morning to the most laborious training exercises.

Around Tarascon is a promenade planted with trees which, in the local dictionary, is called the "Tour de Ville." Every Sunday afternoon, the Tarasconese, who, in spite of their imagination, are a people of routine, make the tour of their town, and always in the same direction. Tartarin now exercised himself by making it eight times, ten times, of a morning, and often reversed the way. He walked, his hands behind his back, with short-mountain-steps, both slow and sure, till the shopkeepers, alarmed by this infraction of local habits, were lost in suppositions of all possible kinds.

At home, in his exotic garden, he practised the art of leaping crevasses, by jumping over the basin in which a few gold-fish were swimming about among the water-weeds. On two occasions he fell in, and was forced to change his clothes. Such mishaps inspired him only the more, and, being subject to vertigo, he practised walking on the narrow masonry round the edge of the water, to the terror of his old servant-woman, who understood nothing of these performances.

During this time, he ordered, *in Avignon*, from an excellent locksmith, crampons of the Whymper pattern, and a Kennedy ice-axe; also he procured himself a reed-wick lamp, two impermeable coverlets, and two hundred feet of rope of his own invention, woven with iron wire.

The arrival of these different articles from Avignon, the mysterious goings and comings which their construction required, puzzled the Taras-conese much, and it was generally said about town: "The president is preparing a stroke." But what? Something grand, you may be sure, for, in the beautiful words of the brave and sententious Commander Bravida, retired captain of equipment, who never spoke except in apothegms: "Eagles hunt no flies."

With his closest intimates Tartarin remained impenetrable. Only, at the sessions of the Club, they noticed the quivering of his voice and the lightning flash of his eyes whenever he addressed Costecalde--the indirect cause of this new expedition, the dangers and fatigues of which became more pronounced to his mind the nearer he approached it. The unfortunate man did not attempt to disguise them; in fact he took so black a view of the matter that he thought it indispensable to set his affairs in order, to write those last wishes, the expression of which is so trying to the Tarasconese, lovers of life, that most of them die intestate.

On a radiant morning in June, beneath a cloudless arched and splendid sky, the door of his study open upon the neat little garden with its gravelled paths, where the exotic plants stretched forth their motionless lilac shadows, where the fountain tinkled its silvery note 'mid the merry shouts of the Savoyards, playing at marbles before the gate, behold Tartarin! in Turkish slippers, wide flannel under-garments, easy in body, his pipe at hand, reading aloud as he wrote the words:--

"This is my last will and testament."

Ha! one may have one's heart in the right place and solidly hooked there, but these are cruel moments. Nevertheless, neither his hand nor his voice trembled while he distributed among his fellow-citizens all the ethnographical riches piled in his little home, carefully dusted and preserved in immaculate order.

"To the Club of the Alpines, my baobab (***arbos gigantea***) to stand on the chimney-piece of the hall of sessions;"

To Bravida, his carbines, revolvers, hunting knives, Malay krishes, tomahawks, and other murderous weapons;

To Excourbanies, all his pipes, calumets, narghiles, and pipelets for smoking kif and opium;

To Costecalde--yes, Costecalde himself had his legacy--the famous poisoned arrows (Do not touch).

Perhaps beneath this gift was the secret hope that the traitor would touch and die; but nothing of the kind was exhaled by the will, which closed with the following words, of a divine meekness:

"I beg my dear Alpinists not to forget their president... I wish them to forgive my enemy as I have forgiven him, although it is he who has caused my death..."

Here Tartarin was forced to stop, blinded by a flood of tears. For a minute he beheld himself crushed, lying in fragments at the foot of a high mountain, his shapeless remains gathered up in a barrow, and brought back to Tarascon. Oh, the power of that Provencal imagination! he was present at his own funeral; he heard the lugubrious chants, and the talk above his grave: "Poor Tartarin, ***pechere!***" and, mingling with the crowd of his faithful friends, he wept for himself.

But immediately after, the sight of the sun streaming into his study and glittering on the weapons and pipes in their usual order, the song of that thread of a fountain in the middle of the garden recalled him to the actual state of things. ***Differemment***, why die? Why go, even? Who obliged him? What foolish vanity! Risk his life for a presidential chair and three letters!..

'Twas a passing weakness, and it lasted no longer than any other. At the end of five minutes the will was finished, signed, the flourish added, sealed with an enormous black seal, and the great man had concluded his last preparations for departure.

Once more had the warren Tartarin triumphed over the cabbage Tartarin. It could be said of the Tarasconese hero, as was said of Turenne: "His body was not always willing to go into battle, but his will led him there in spite of himself."

The evening of that same day, as the last stroke of ten was sounding from the tower of the town-hall, the streets being already deserted, a man, after brusquely slamming a door, glided along through the darkened town, where nothing lighted the fronts of the houses, save the hanging-lamps of the streets and the pink and green bottles of the pharmacy Bezuquet, which projected their reflections on the pavement, together with a silhouette of the apothecary himself resting his elbows on his desk and sound asleep on the Codex;--a little nap, which he took every evening from nine to ten, to make himself, so he said, the fresher at night for those who might need his services. That, between ourselves, was a mere tarasconade, for no one ever waked him at night, in fact he himself had cut the bell-wire, in order that he might sleep more tranquilly.

Suddenly Tartarin entered, loaded with rugs, carpet-bag in hand, and so pale, so discomposed, that the apothecary, with that fiery local imagination from which the pharmacy was no preservative, jumped to the conclusion of some alarming misadventure and was terrified. "Unhappy man!" he cried, "what is it?.. you are poisoned?.. Quick! quick! some ipeca..."

And he sprang forward, bustling among his bottles. To stop him, Tartarin was forced to catch him round the waist. "Listen to me, *que diable!*" and his voice grated with the vexation of an actor whose entrance has been made to miss fire. As soon as the apothecary was rendered motionless behind the counter by an iron wrist, Tartarin said in a low voice:--

"Are we alone, Bezuquet?"

"*Be*! yes," ejaculated the other, looking about in vague alarm... "Pascalon has gone to bed." [Pascalon was his pupil.] "Mamma too; why do you ask?"

"Shut the shutters," commanded Tartarin, without replying; "we might be seen from without."

Bezuquet obeyed, trembling. An old bachelor, living with his mother, whom he never quitted, he had all the gentleness and timidity of a girl, contrasting oddly with his swarthy skin, his hairy lips, his great hooked nose above a spreading moustache; in short, the head of an Algerine pirate before the conquest. These antitheses are frequent in Tarascon, where heads have too much character, Roman or Saracen, heads with the expression of models for a school of design, but quite out of place in bourgeois trades among the manners and customs of a little town.

For instance, Excourbanies, who has all the air of a *conquistador*, companion of Pizarro, rolls flaming eyes in selling haberdashery to induce the purchase of two sous' worth of thread. And Bezuquet, labelling liquorice and *sirupus gummi*, resembles an old sea-rover of the Barbary coast.

When the shutters were put up and secured by iron bolts and transversal bars, "Listen, Ferdinand…" said Tartarin, who was fond of calling people by their Christian names. And thereupon he unbosomed himself, emptied his heart full of bitterness at the ingratitude of his compatriots, related the manoeuvres of "Cock-leg," the trick about to be played upon him at the coming elections, and the manner in which he expected to parry the blow.

Before all else, the matter must be kept very secret; it must not be revealed until the moment when success was assured, unless some unforeseen accident, one of those frightful catastrophes--"Hey, Bezuquet! don't whistle in that way when I talk to you."

This was one of the apothecary's ridiculous habits. Not talkative by nature (a negative quality seldom met with in Tarascon, and which won him this confidence of the president), his thick lips, always in the form of an O, had a habit of perpetually whistling that gave him an appearance of laughing in the nose of the world, even on the gravest occasions.

So that, while the hero made allusion to his possible death, saying, as he laid upon the counter a large sealed envelope, "This is my last will and testament, Bezuquet; it is you whom I have chosen as testamentary executor…" "Hui… hui… hui…" whistled the apothecary, carried away by his mania, while at heart he was deeply moved and fully conscious of the grandeur of his role.

Then, the hour of departure being at hand, he desired to drink to the enterprise, "something good, *que?* a glass of the elixir of Garus, hey?" After several closets had been opened and searched, he remembered that mamma had the keys of the Garus. To get them it would be necessary to awaken her and tell who was there. The elixir was therefore changed to a glass of the *sirop de Calabre*, a summer drink, inoffensive and modest, which Bezuquet invented, advertising it in the *Forum* as follows: Sirop de Calabre, ten sous a bottle, including the glass (verre). "Sirop de Cadavre, including the worms (*vers*)," said that infernal Costecalde, who spat upon all success. But, after all, that horrid play upon words only served to swell the sale, and the Tarasconese to this day delight in their **sirop de cadavre**.

Libations made and a few last words exchanged, they embraced, Bezuquet whistling as usual in his moustache, adown which rolled great tears.

"Adieu, **au mouain**"... said Tartarin in a rough tone, feeling that he was about to weep himself, and as the shutter of the door had been lowered the hero was compelled to creep out of the pharmacy on his hands and knees.

This was one of the trials of the journey now about to begin.

Three days later he landed in Vitznau at the foot of the Rigi. As the mountain for his debut, the Rigi had attracted him by its low altitude (5900 feet, about ten times that of Mount Terrible, the highest of the Alpines) and also on account of the splendid panorama to be seen from the summit--the Bernese Alps marshalled in line, all white and rosy, around the lakes, awaiting the moment when the great ascensionist should cast his ice-axe upon one of them.

Certain of being recognized on the way and perhaps followed--'t was a foible of his to believe that throughout all France his fame was as great and popular as it was at Tarascon--he had made a great detour before entering Switzerland and did not don his accoutrements until after he had crossed the frontier. Luckily for him; for never could his armament have been contained in one French railway-carriage.

But, however convenient the Swiss compartments might be, the Alpinist, hampered with utensils to which he was not, as yet, accustomed, crushed toe-nails with his crampons, harpooned travellers who came in his way with the point of his alpenstock, and wherever he went, in the stations, the steamers, and the hotel salons, he excited as much amazement as he did maledictions, avoidance, and angry looks, which he could not explain to himself though his affectionate and communicative nature suffered from them. To complete his discomfort, the sky was always gray, with flocks of clouds and a driving rain.

It rained at Bale, on the little white houses, washed and rewashed by the hands of a maid and the waters of heaven. It rained at Lucerne, on the quay where the trunks and boxes appeared to be saved, as it were, from shipwreck, and when he arrived at the station of Vitznau, on the shore of the lake of the Four-Cantons, the same deluge was descending on the verdant slopes of the Rigi, straddled by inky clouds and striped with torrents that leaped from rock to rock in cascades of misty sleet, bringing down as they came the loose stones and the pine-needles. Never had Tartarin seen so much water.

He entered an inn and ordered a **cafe au lait** with honey and butter, the only really good things he had as yet tasted during his journey. Then, reinvigorated, and his beard sticky with honey, cleaned on a corner of his napkin, he prepared to attempt his first ascension.

"**Et autremain**" he asked, as he shifted his knapsack, "how long does it take to ascend the Rigi?"

"One hour, one hour and a quarter, monsieur; but make haste about it; the train is just starting."

"A train upon the Rigi!.. you are joking!.."

Through the leaded panes of the tavern window he was shown the train that was really starting. Two great covered carriages, windowless, pushed by a locomotive with a short, corpulent chimney, in shape like a saucepan, a monstrous insect, clinging to the mountain and clambering, breathless up its vertiginous slopes.

The two Tartarins, cabbage and warren, both, at the same instant, revolted at the thought of going up in that hideous mechanism. One of them thought it ridiculous to climb the Alps in a lift; as for the other, those aerial bridges on which the track was laid, with the prospect of a fall of 4000 feet at the slightest derailment, inspired him with all sorts of lamentable reflections, justified by the little cemetery of Vitzgau, the white tombs of which lay huddled together at the foot of the slope, like linen spread out to bleach in the yard of a wash-house. Evidently the cemetery is there by way of precaution, so that, in case of accident, the travellers may drop on the very spot.

"I'll go afoot," the valiant Tarasconese said to himself; "'twill exercise me... zou!"

And he started, wholly preoccupied with manoeuvring his alpenstock in presence of the staff of the hotel, collected about the door and shouting directions to him about the path, to which he did not listen. He first followed an ascending road, paved with large irregular, pointed stones like a lane at the South, and bordered with wooden gutters to carry off the rains.

To right and left were great orchards, fields of rank, lush grass crossed by the same wooden conduits for irrigation through hollowed trunks of trees. All this made a constant rippling from top to bottom of the mountain, and every time that the ice-axe of the Alpinist became hooked as he walked along in the lower branches of an oak or a walnut-tree, his cap crackled as if beneath the nozzle of a watering-pot.

"Diou! what a lot of water!" sighed the man of the South. But it was much worse when the pebbly path abruptly ceased and he was forced to puddle along in the torrent or jump from rock to rock to save his gaiters. Then a shower joined in, penetrating, steady, and seeming to get colder the higher he went. When he stopped to recover breath he could hear nothing else than a vast noise of waters in which he seemed to be sunk, and he saw, as he turned round, the clouds descending into the lake in delicate long filaments of spun glass through which the chalets of Vitznau shone like freshly varnished toys.

Men and children passed him with lowered heads and backs bent beneath hods of white-wood, containing provisions for some villa or **pension**, the balconies of which could be distinguished on the slopes. "Rigi-Kulm?" asked Tartarin, to be sure he was heading in the right direction. But his extraordinary equipment, especially, that knitted muffler which masked his face, cast terror along the way, and all whom he addressed only opened their eyes wide and hastened their steps without replying.

Soon these encounters became rare. The last human being whom he saw was an old woman washing her linen in the hollowed trunk of a tree under the shelter of an enormous red umbrella, planted in the ground.

"Rigi-Kulm?" asked the Alpinist.

The old woman raised an idiotic, cadaverous face, with a goitre swaying upon her throat as large as the rustic bell of a Swiss cow. Then, after gazing at him for a long time, she was seized with inextinguishable laughter, which stretched her mouth from ear to ear, wrinkled up the corners of her little eyes, and every time she opened them the sight of Tartarin, planted before her with his ice-axe on his shoulder, redoubled her joy.

"*Tron de l'air!*" growled the Tarasconese, "lucky for her that she's a woman..." Snorting with anger, he continued his way and lost it in a pine-wood, where his boots slipped on the oozing moss.

Beyond this point the landscape changed. No more paths, or trees, or pastures. Gloomy, denuded slopes, great boulders of rock which he scaled on his knees for fear of falling; sloughs full of yellow mud, which he crossed slowly, feeling before him with his alpenstock and lifting his feet like a knife-grinder. At every moment he looked at the compass hanging to his broad watch-ribbon; but whether it were the altitude or the variations of the temperature, the needle seemed untrue. And how could he find his bearings in a thick yellow fog that hindered him from seeing ten steps about him--steps that were now, within a moment, covered with an icy glaze that made the ascent more difficult.

Suddenly he stopped; the ground whitened vaguely before him... Look out for your eyes!..

He had come to the region of snows...

Immediately he pulled out his spectacles, took them from their case, and settled them securely on his nose. The moment was a solemn one. Slightly agitated, yet proud all the same, it seemed to Tar-tarin that in one bound he had risen 3000 feet toward the summits and his greatest dangers.

He now advanced with more precaution, dreaming of crevasses and fissures such as the books tell of, and cursing in the depths of his heart those people at the inn who advised him to mount straight and take no guide. After all, perhaps he had mistaken the mountain! More than six hours had he tramped, and the Rigi required only three. The wind blew, a chilling wind that whirled the snow in that crepuscular fog.

Night was about to overtake him. Where find a hut? or even a projecting rock to shelter him? All of a sudden, he saw before his nose on the arid, naked plain a species of wooden chalet, bearing, on a long placard in gigantic type, these letters, which he deciphered with difficulty: PHO... TO... GRA... PHIE DU RI... GI KULM. At the same instant the vast hotel with its three hundred windows loomed up before him between the great lamp-posts, the globes of which were now being lighted in the fog.

III.

An alarm on the Rigi. "Keep cool! Keep cool!" The Alpine horn. What Tartarin saw, on awaking, in his looking-glass, Perplexity. A guide is ordered by telephone.

"Ques aco?.. Qui vive?" cried Tartarin, ears alert and eyes straining hard into the darkness.

Feet were running through the hotel, doors were slamming, breathless voices were crying: "Make haste! make haste!.." while without was ringing what seemed to be a trumpet-call, as flashes of flame illumined both panes and curtains.

Fire!..

At a bound he was out of bed, shod, clothed, and running headlong down the staircase, where the gas still burned and a rustling swarm of *misses* were descending, with hair put up in haste, and they themselves swathed in shawls and red woollen jackets, or anything else that came to hand as they jumped out of bed.

Tartarin, to fortify himself and also to reassure the young ladies, cried out, as he rushed on, hustling everybody: "Keep cool! Keep cool!" in the voice of a gull, pallid, distraught, one of those voices that we hear in dreams sending chills down the back of the bravest man. Now, can you understand those young *misses*, who laughed as they looked at him and seemed to think it very funny? Girls have no notion of danger, at that age!..

Happily, the old diplomatist came along behind them, very cursorily clothed in a top-coat below which appeared his white drawers with trailing ends of tape-string.

Here was a man, at last!..

Tartarin ran to him waving his arms: "Ah! Monsieur le baron, what a disaster!.. Do you know about it?.. Where is it?.. How did it take?.."

"Who? What?" stuttered the terrified baron, not understanding.

"Why, the fire..."

"What fire?.."

The poor man's countenance was so inexpressibly vacant and stupid that Tartarin abandoned him and rushed away abruptly to "organize help..."

"Help!" repeated the baron, and after him four or five waiters, sound asleep on their feet in the antechamber, looked at one another completely bewildered and echoed, "Help!.."

At the first step that Tartarin made out-of-doors he saw his error. Not the slightest conflagration! Only savage cold, and pitchy darkness, scarcely lighted by the resinous torches that were being carried hither and thither, casting on the snow long, blood-coloured traces.

On the steps of the portico, a performer on the Alpine horn was bellowing his modulated moan, that monotonous *ranz des vaches* on three notes, with which the Rigi-Kulm is wont to waken the worshippers of the sun and announce to them the rising of their star.

It is said that it shows itself, sometimes, on rising, at the extreme top of the mountain behind the hotel. To get his bearings, Tartarin had only to follow the long peal of the misses' laughter which now went past him. But he walked more slowly, still full of sleep and his legs heavy with his six hours' climb.

"Is that you, Manilof?.." said a clear voice from the darkness, the voice of a woman. "Help me... I have lost my shoe."

He recognized at once the foreign warble of his pretty little neighbour at the dinner-table, whose delicate silhouette he now saw in the first pale gleam of the coming sun.

"It is not Manilof, mademoiselle, but if I can be useful to you..."

She gave a little cry of surprise and alarm as she made a recoiling gesture that Tartarin did not perceive, having already stooped to feel about the short and crackling grass around them.

"*Te, pardi!* here it is!" he cried joyfully. He shook the dainty shoe which the snow had powdered, and putting a knee to earth, most gallantly in the snow and the dampness, he asked, for all reward, the honour of replacing it on Cinderella's foot.

She, more repellent than in the tale, replied with a very curt "no;" and endeavoured, by hopping on one foot, to reinstate her silk stocking in its little bronze shoe; but in that she could never have succeeded without the help of the hero, who was greatly moved by feeling for an instant that delicate hand upon his shoulder.

"You have good eyes," she said, by way of thanks as they now walked side by side, and feeling their way.

"The habit of watching for game, mademoiselle."

"Ah! you are a sportsman?"

She said it with an incredulous, satirical, accent Tartarin had only to name himself in order to convince her, but, like the bearers of all illustrious names, he preferred discretion, coquetry. So, wishing to graduate the surprise, he answered:--

"I am a sportsman, *effectivemain*."

She continued in the same tone of irony:--

"And what game do you prefer to hunt?"

"The great carnivora, wild beasts..." uttered Tartarin, thinking to dazzle her.

"Do you find many on the Rigi?"

Always gallant, and ready in reply, Tartarin was about to say that on the Rigi he had so far met none but gazelles, when his answer was suddenly cut short by the appearance of two shadows, who called out:--

"Sonia!.. Sonia!.."

"I'm coming," she said, and turning to Tartarin, whose eyes, now accustomed to the darkness, could distinguish her pale and pretty face beneath her mantle, she added, this time seriously:--

"You have undertaken a dangerous enterprise, my good man... take care you do not leave your bones here."

So saying, she instantly disappeared in the darkness with her companions.

Later, the threatening intonation that emphasized those words was fated to trouble the imagination of the Southerner; but now, he was simply vexed at the term "good man," cast upon his elderly embonpoint, and also at the abrupt departure of the young girl just at the moment when he was about to name himself, and enjoy her stupefaction.

He made a few steps in the direction the group had taken, hearing a confused murmur, with coughs and sneezes, of the clustering tourists waiting impatiently for the rising of the sun, the most vigorous among them having climbed to a little belvedere, the steps of which, wadded with snow, could be whitely distinguished in the vanishing darkness.

A gleam was beginning to light the Orient, saluted by a fresh blast from the Alpine horn, and that "Ah!!" of relief, always heard in theatres when the third bell raises the curtain.

Slight as a ray through a shutter, this gleam, nevertheless, enlarged the horizon, but, at the same moment a fog, opaque and yellow, rose from the valley, a steam that grew more thick, more penetrating as the day advanced. 'T was a veil between the scene and the spectators.

All hope was now renounced of the gigantic effects predicted in the guide-books. On the other hand, the heteroclite array of the dancers of the night before, torn from their slumbers, appeared in fantastic and ridiculous outline like the shades of a magic lantern; shawls, rugs, and even bed-quilts wrapped around them. Under varied headgear, nightcaps of silk or cotton, broad-brimmed female hats, turbans, fur caps with ear-pads, were haggard faces, swollen faces, heads of shipwrecked beings cast upon a desert island in mid-ocean, watching for a sail in the offing with staring eyes.

But nothing--everlastingly nothing!

Nevertheless, certain among them strove, in a gush of good-will, to distinguish the surrounding summits, and, on the top of the belvedere could be heard the clucking of the Peruvian family, pressing around a big devil, wrapped to his feet in a checked ulster, who was pointing out imperturbably, the invisible panorama of the Bernese Alps, naming in a loud voice the peaks that were lost in the fog.

"You see on the left the Finsteraarhorn, thirteen thousand seven hundred and ninety-five feet high... the Schreckhorn, the Wetterhorn, the Monk, the Jungfrau, the elegant proportions of which I especially point out to these young ladies..."

"***Be! ve!*** there's one who does n't lack cheek!" thought Tartarin; then, on reflection, he added: "I know that voice, ***au mouain.***"

He recognized the accent, that accent of the South, distinguishable from afar like garlic; but, quite preoccupied in finding again his fair Unknown, he did not pause, and continued to inspect the groups--without result. She must have reentered the hotel, as they all did now, weary with standing about, shivering, to no purpose, so that presently no one remained on the cold and desolate plateau of that gray dawn but Tartarin and the Alpine horn-player, who continued to blow a melancholy note through his huge instrument, like a dog baying the moon.

He was a short old man, with a long beard, wearing a Tyrolese hat adorned with green woollen tassels that hung down upon his back and, in letters of gold, the words (common to all the hats and caps in the service of the hotel) **Regina Montium**. Tartarin went up to give him a pourboire, as he had seen all the other tourists do. "Let us go to bed again, my old friend," he said, tapping him on the shoulder with Tarasconese familiarity. "A fine humbug, *que!* the sunrise on the Rigi."

The old man continued to blow into his horn, concluding his ritornelle in three notes with a mute laugh that wrinkled the corners of his eyes and shook the green glands of his head-gear.

Tartarin, in spite of all, did not regret his night. That meeting with the pretty blonde repaid him for his loss of sleep, for, though nigh upon fifty, he still had a warm heart, a romantic imagination, a glowing hearthstone of life. Returning to bed, and shutting his eyes to make himself go to sleep, he fancied he felt in his hand that dainty little shoe, and heard again the gentle call of the fair young girl: "Is it you, Manilof?"

Sonia... what a pretty name!.. She was certainly Russian; and those young men were travelling with her; friends of her brother, no doubt.

Then all grew hazy; the pretty face in its golden curls joined the other floating visions,--Rigi slopes, cascades like plumes of feathers,--and soon the heroic breathing of the great man, sonorous and rhythmical, filled the little room and the greater part of the long corridor...

The next morning, before descending at the first gong for breakfast, Tartarin was about to make sure that his beard was well brushed, and that he himself did not look too badly in his Alpine costume, when, all of a sudden, he quivered. Before him, open, and gummed to his looking-glass by two wafers, was an anonymous letter, containing the following threats:--

"Devil of a Frenchman, your queer old clothes do not conceal you. You are forgiven once more for this attempt; but if you cross our path again, beware!"

Bewildered, he read this two or three times over without understanding it. Of whom, of what must he beware? How came that letter there? Evidently during his sleep; for he did not see it on returning from his auroral promenade. He rang for the maid on duty; a fat, white face, all pitted with the small-pox, a perfect gruyere cheese, from which nothing intelligible could be drawn, except that she was of "bon famille," and never entered the rooms of the gentlemen unless they were there.

"A queer thing, ***au mouain***," thought Tartarin, turning and returning the letter, and much impressed by it. For a moment the name of Coste-calde crossed his mind,--Costecalde, informed of his projects of ascension, and endeavouring to prevent them by manoeuvres and threats. On reflection, this appeared to him unlikely, and he ended by persuading himself that the letter was a joke... perhaps those little misses who had laughed at him so heartily... they are so free, those English and American young girls!

The second breakfast gong sounded. He put the letter in his pocket: "After all, we'll soon see..." and the formidable grimace with which he accompanied that reflection showed the heroism of his soul.

Fresh surprise when he sat down to table. Instead of his pretty neighbour, "whom Love had curled with gold," he perceived the vulture throat of an old Englishwoman, whose long lappets swept the cloth. It was rumoured about him that the young lady and her companions had left the hotel by one of the early morning trains.

"'***Cri nom!*** I'm fooled..." exclaimed aloud the Italian tenor, who, the evening before, had so rudely signified to Tartarin that he could not speak French. He must have learned it in a single night! The tenor rose, threw down his napkin, and hurried away, leaving the Southerner completely nonplussed.

Of all the guests of the night before, none now remained but himself. That is always so on the Rigi-Kulm; no one stays there more than twenty-four hours. In other respects the scene was invariably the same; the compote-dishes in files divided the factions. But on this particular morning the Rices triumphed by a great majority, reinforced by certain illustrious personages, and the Prunes did not, as they say, have it all their own way.

Tartarin, without taking sides with one or the other, went up to his room before the dessert, buckled his bag, and asked for his bill. He had had enough of ***Regina Montium*** and its dreary table d'hote of deaf mutes.

Abruptly recalled to his Alpine madness by the touch of his ice-axe, his crampons, and the rope in which he rewound himself, he burned to attack a real mountain, a summit deprived of a lift and a photographer. He hesitated between the Finsteraarhorn, as being the highest, and the Jungfrau, whose pretty name of virginal whiteness made him think more than once of the little Russian.

Ruminating on these alternatives while they made out his bill, he amused himself in the vast, lugubrious, silent hall of the hotel by looking at the coloured photographs hanging to the walls, representing glaciers, snowy slopes, famous and perilous mountain passes: here, were ascensionists in file, like ants on a quest, creeping along an icy *arete* sharply defined and blue; farther on was a deep crevasse, with glaucous sides, over which was thrown a ladder, and a lady crossing it on her knees, with an abbe after her raising his cassock.

The Alpinist of Tarascon, both hands on his ice-axe, had never, as yet, had an idea of such difficulties; he would have to meet them, *pas mouain!*..

Suddenly he paled fearfully.

In a black frame, an engraving from the famous drawing of Gustave Dore, reproducing the catastrophe on the Matterhorn, met his eye. Four human bodies on the flat of their backs or stomachs were coming headlong down the almost perpendicular slope of a *neve*, with extended arms and clutching hands, seeking the broken rope which held this string of lives, and only served to drag them down to death in the gulf where the mass was to fall pell-mell, with ropes, axes, veils, and all the gay outfit of Alpine ascension, grown suddenly tragic.

"Awful!" cried Tartarin, speaking aloud in his horror.

A very civil maitre d'hotel heard the exclamation, and thought best to reassure him. Accidents of that nature, he said, were becoming very rare: the essential thing was to commit no imprudence and, above all, to procure good guides.

Tartarin asked if he could be told of one there, "with confidence..." Not that he himself had any fear, but it was always best to have a sure man.

The waiter reflected, with an important air, twirling his moustache. "With confidence?.. Ah! if monsieur had only spoken sooner; we had a man here this morning who was just the thing... the courier of that Peruvian family..."

"He understands the mountain?" said Tartarin, with a knowing air.

"Oh, yes, monsieur, all the mountains, in Switzerland, Savoie, Tyrol, India, in fact, the whole world; he has done them all, he knows them all, he can tell you all about them, and that's something!.. I think he might easily be induced... With a man like that a child could go anywhere without danger."

"Where is he? How could I find him?"

"At the Kaltbad, monsieur, preparing the rooms for his party... I could telephone to him."

A telephone! on the Rigi!

That was the climax. But Tartarin could no longer be amazed.

Five minutes later the man returned bringing an answer.

The courier of the Peruvian party had just started for the Tellsplatte, where he would certainly pass the night.

The Tellsplatte is a memorial chapel, to which pilgrimages are made in honour of William Tell. Some persons go there to see the mural pictures which a famous painter of Bale has lately executed in the chapel...

As it only took by boat an hour or an hour and a half to reach the place, Tartarin did not hesitate. It would make him lose a day, but he owed it to himself to render that homage to William Tell, for whom he had always felt a peculiar predilection. And, besides, what a chance if he could there pick up this marvellous guide and induce him to do the Jungfrau with him.

Forward, *zou!*

He paid his bill, in which the setting and the rising sun were reckoned as extras, also the candles and the attendance. Then, still preceded by the rattle of his metals, which sowed surprise and terror on his way, he went to the railway station, because to descend the Rigi as he had ascended it, on foot, would have been lost time, and, really, it was doing too much honour to that very artificial mountain.

IV.

On the boat. It rains. The Tarasconese hero salutes the Ashes. The truth about William Tell. Disillusion. Tartarin of Tarascon never existed. "Te! Bompard."

He had left the snows of the Rigi-Kulm; down below, on the lake, he returned to rain, fine, close, misty, a vapour of water through which the mountains stumped themselves in, graduating in the distance to the form of clouds.

The "Foehn" whistled, raising white caps on the lake where the gulls, flying low, seemed borne upon the waves; one might have thought one's self on the open ocean.

Tartarin recalled to mind his departure from the port of Marseilles, fifteen years earlier, when he started to hunt the lion--that spotless sky, dazzling with silvery light, that sea so blue, blue as the water of dye-works, blown back by the mistral in sparkling white saline crystals, the bugles of the forts and the bells of all the steeples echoing joy, rapture, sun--the fairy world of a first journey.

What a contrast to this black dripping wharf, almost deserted, on which were seen, through the mist as through a sheet of oiled paper, a few passengers wrapped in ulsters and formless india-rubber garments, and the helmsman standing motionless, muffled in his hooded cloak, his manner grave and sibylline, behind this notice printed in three languages:--

"Forbidden to speak to the man at the wheel."

Very useless caution, for nobody spoke on board the "Winkelried," neither on deck, nor in the first and second saloons crowded with lugubrious-looking passengers, sleeping, reading, yawning, pell-mell, with their smaller packages scattered on the seats--the sort of scene we imagine that a batch of exiles on the morning after a coup-d'Etat might present.

From time to time the hoarse bellow of the steam-pipe announced the arrival of the boat at a stopping-place. A noise of steps, and of baggage dragged about the deck. The shore, looming through the fog, came nearer and showed its slopes of a sombre green, its villas shivering amid inundated groves, files of poplars flanking the muddy roads along which sumptuous hotels were formed in line with their names in letters of gold upon their facades, Hotel Meyer, Mueller, du Lac, etc., where heads, bored with existence, made themselves visible behind the streaming window-panes.

The wharf was reached, the passengers disembarked and went upward, all equally muddy, soaked, and silent. 'Twas a coming and going of umbrellas and omnibuses, quickly vanishing. Then a great beating of the wheels, churning up the water with their paddles, and the shore retreated, becoming once more a misty landscape with its ***pensions*** Meyer, Mueller, du Lac, etc., the windows of which, opened for an instant, gave fluttering handkerchiefs to view from every floor, and outstretched arms that seemed to say: "Mercy! pity! take us, take us... if you only knew!.."

At times the "Winkelried" crossed on its way some other steamer with its name in black letters on its white paddle-box: "Germania.".. "Guillaume Tell"... The same lugubrious deck, the same refracting caoutchoucs, the same most lamentable pleasure trip as that of the other phantom vessel going its different way, and the same heart-broken glances exchanged from deck to deck.

And to say that those people travelled for enjoyment! and that all those boarders in the Hotels du Lac, Meyer, and Mueller were captives for pleasure!

Here, as on the Rigi-Kulm, the thing that above all suffocated Tartarin, agonized him, froze him, even more than the cold rain and the murky sky, was the utter impossibility of talking. True, he had again met faces that he knew--the member of the Jockey Club with his niece (h'm! h'm!..), the academician Astier-Rehu, and the Bonn Professor Schwanthaler, those two implacable enemies condemned to live side by side for a month manacled to the itinerary of a Cook's Circular, and others. But none of these illustrious Prunes would recognize the Tarasconese Alpinist, although his mountain muffler, his metal utensils, his ropes in saltire, distinguished him from others, and marked him in a manner that was quite peculiar. They all seemed ashamed of the night before, and the inexplicable impulse communicated to them by the fiery ardour of that fat man.

Mme. Schwanthaler, alone, approached her partner, with the rosy, laughing face of a plump little fairy, and taking her skirt in her two fingers as if to suggest a minuet. "Ballir... dantsir... very choli..." remarked the good lady. Was this a memory that she evoked, or a temptation that she offered? At any rate, as she did not let go of him, Tartarin, to escape her pertinacity, went up on deck, preferring to be soaked to the skin rather than be made ridiculous.

And it rained!.. and the sky was dirty!.. To complete his gloom, a whole squad of the Salvation Army, who had come aboard at Beckenried, a dozen stout girls with stolid faces, in navy-blue gowns and Greenaway bonnets, were grouped under three enormous scarlet umbrellas, and were singing verses, accompanied on the accordion by a man, a sort of David-la-Gamme, tall and fleshless with crazy eyes.

These sharp, flat, discordant voices, like the cry of gulls, rolled dragging, drawling through the rain and the black smoke of the engine which the wind beat down upon the deck. Never had Tartarin heard anything so lamentable.

At Bruennen the squad landed, leaving the pockets of the other travellers swollen with pious little tracts; and almost immediately after the songs and the accordion of these poor larvae ceased, the sky began to clear and patches of blue were seen.

They now entered the lake of Uri, closed in and darkened by lofty, untrodden mountains, and the tourists pointed out to each other, on the right at the foot of the Seelisberg, the field of Gruetli, where Melchtal, Fuerst, and Stauffacher made oath to deliver their country.

Tartarin, with much emotion, took off his cap, paying no attention to environing amazement, and waved it in the air three times, to do honour to the ashes of those heroes. A few of the passengers mistook his purpose, and politely returned his bow.

The engine at last gave a hoarse roar, its echo repercussioning from cliff to cliff of the narrow space. The notice hung out on deck before each new landing-place (as they do at public balls to vary the country dances) announced the Tells-platte.

They arrived.

The chapel is situated just five minutes' walk from the landing, at the edge of the lake, on the very rock to which William Tell sprang, during the tempest, from Gessler's boat. It was to Tartarin a most delightful emotion to tread, as he followed the travellers of the Circular Cook along the lakeside, that historic soil, to recall and live again the principal episodes of the great drama which he knew as he did his own life.

From his earliest years, William Tell had been his type. When, in the Bezuquet pharmacy, they played the game of preference, each person writing secretly on folded slips the poet, the tree, the odour, the hero, the woman he preferred, one of the papers invariably ran thus:--

"Tree preferred? .... the baobab.
Odour? .... gunpowder.
Writer? .... Fenimore Cooper.
What I would prefer to be .. William Tell."

And every voice in the pharmacy cried out: "That's Tartarin!"

Imagine, therefore, how happy he was and how his heart was beating as he stood before that memorial chapel raised to a hero by the gratitude of a whole people. It seemed to him that William Tell in person, still dripping with the waters of the lake, his crossbow and his arrows in hand, was about to open the door to him.

"No entrance... I am at work... This is not the day..." cried a loud voice from within, made louder by the sonority of the vaulted roof.

"Monsieur Astier-Rehu, of the French Academy..."

"Herr Doctor Professor Schwanthaler..."

"Tartarin of Tarascon..."

In the arch above the portal, perched upon a scaffolding, appeared a half-length of the painter in working-blouse, palette in hand.

"My *famulus* will come down and open to you, messieurs," he said with respectful intonations.

"I was sure of it, ***pardi!***" thought Tartarin; "I had only to name myself."

However, he had the good taste to stand aside modestly, and only entered after all the others.

The painter, superb fellow, with the gilded, ruddy head of an artist of the Renaissance, received his visitors on the wooden steps which led to the temporary staging put up for the purpose of painting the roof. The frescos, representing the principal episodes in the life of William Tell, were finished, all but one, namely: the scene of the apple in the market-place of Altorf. On this he was now at work, and his young *famulus*, as he called him, feet and legs bare under a toga of the middle ages, and his hair archangelically arranged, was posing as the son of William Tell.

All these archaic personages, red, green, yellow, blue, made taller than nature in narrow streets and under the posterns of the period, intended, of course, to be seen at a distance, impressed the spectators rather sadly. However, they were there to admire, and they admired. Besides, none of them knew anything.

"I consider that a fine characterization," said the pontifical Astier-Rehu, carpet-bag in hand.

And Schwanthaler, a camp-stool under his arm, not willing to be behindhand, quoted two verses of Schiller, most of it remaining in his flowing beard. Then the ladies exclaimed, and for a time nothing was heard but:--

"Schoen!.. schoen..."

"Yes... lovely..."

"Exquisite! delicious!.."

One might have thought one's self at a confectioner's.

Abruptly a voice broke forth, rending with the ring of a trumpet that composed silence.

"Badly shouldered, I tell you... That crossbow is not in place..."

Imagine the stupor of the painter in presence of this exorbitant Alpinist, who, alpenstock in hand and ice-axe on his shoulder, risking the annihilation of somebody at each of his many evolutions, was demonstrating to him by A + B that the motions of his William Tell were not correct.

"I know what I am talking about, *au mouain*... I beg you to believe it..."

"Who are you?"

"Who am I!" exclaimed the Alpinist, now thoroughly vexed... So it was not to him that the door was opened; and drawing himself up he said: "Go ask my name of the panthers of the Zaccar, of the lions of Atlas... they will answer you, perhaps."

The company recoiled; there was general alarm.

"But," asked the painter, "in what way is my action wrong?"

"Look at me, *te!*"

Falling into position with a thud of his heels that made the planks beneath them smoke, Tar-tarin, shouldering his ice-axe like a crossbow, stood rigid.

"Superb! He's right... Don't stir..."

Then to the *famulus*: "Quick! a block, charcoal!.."

The fact is, the Tarasconese hero was something worth painting,--squat, round-shouldered, head bent forward, the muffler round his chin like a strap, and his flaming little eye taking aim at the terrified *famulus*.

Imagination, O magic power!.. He thought himself on the marketplace of Altorf, in front of his own child, he, who had never had any; an arrow in his bow, another in his belt to pierce the heart of the tyrant. His conviction became so strong that it conveyed itself to others.

"'T is William Tell himself!.." said the painter, crouched on a stool and driving his sketch with a feverish hand. "Ah! monsieur, why did I not know you earlier? What a model you would have been for me!.."

"Really! then you see some resemblance?" said Tartarin, much flattered, but keeping his pose.

Yes, it was just so that the artist imagined his hero.

"The head, too?"

"Oh! the head, that's no matter..." and the painter stepped back to look at his sketch. "Yes, a virile mask, energetic, just what I wanted--inasmuch as nobody knows anything about William Tell, who probably never existed."

Tartarin dropped the cross-bow from stupefaction.

"*Outre!* {*}.. Never existed!.. What is that you are saying?"

* "Outre" and "boufre" are Tarasconese oaths of mysterious
etymology.

"Ask these gentlemen..."

Astier-Rehu, solemn, his three chins in his white cravat, said: "That is a Danish legend."

"Icelandic.." affirmed Schwanthaler, no less majestic.

"Saxo Grammaticus relates that a valiant archer named Tobe or Paltanoke..."

"Es ist in der Vilkinasaga geschrieben..."

Both together:--

was condemned by the
| dass der Islandische Koenig
King of Denmark Harold | Needing..."
of the Blue Teeth..." |

With staring eyes and arms extended, neither looking at nor comprehending each other, they both talked at once, as if on a rostrum, in the doctoral, despotic tones of professors certain of never being refuted; until, getting angry, they only shouted names: "Justinger of Berne!.. Jean of Winterthur!.."

Little by little, the discussion became general, excited, and furious among the visitors. Umbrellas, camp-stools, and valises were brandished; the unhappy artist, trembling for the safety of his scaffolding, went from one to another imploring peace. When the tempest had abated, he returned to his sketch and looked for his mysterious model, for him whose name the panthers of the Zaccar and the lions of Atlas could alone pronounce; but he was nowhere to be seen; the Alpinist had disappeared.

At that moment he was clambering with furious strides up a little path among beeches and birches that led to the Hotel Tellsplatte, where the courier of the Peruvian family was to pass the night; and under the shock of his deception he was talking to himself in a loud voice and ramming his alpenstock furiously into the sodden ground:--

Never existed! William Tell! William Tell a myth! And it was a painter charged with the duty of decorating the Tellsplatte who said that calmly. He hated him as if for a sacrilege; he hated those learned men, and this denying, demolishing impious age, which respects nothing, neither fame nor grandeur--*coquin de sort!*

And so, two hundred, three hundred years hence, when *Tartarin* was spoken of there would always be Astier-Rehus and Professor Schwanthalers to deny that he ever existed--a Provencal myth! a Barbary legend!.. He stopped, choking with indignation and his rapid climb, and seated himself on a rustic bench.

From there he could see the lake between the branches, and the white walls of the chapel like a new mausoleum. A roaring of steam and the bustle of getting to the wharf announced the arrival of fresh visitors. They collected on the bank, guide-books in hand, and then advanced with thoughtful gestures and extended arms, evidently relating the "legend." Suddenly, by an abrupt revulsion of ideas, the comicality of the whole thing struck him.

He pictured to himself all historical Switzerland living upon this imaginary hero; raising statues and chapels in his honour on the little squares of the little towns, and placing monuments in the museums of the great ones; organizing patriotic fetes, to which everybody rushed, banners displayed, from all the cantons, with banquets, toasts, speeches, hurrahs, songs, and tears swelling all breasts, and this for a great patriot, whom everybody knew had never existed.

Talk of Tarascon indeed! There's a tarasconade for you, the like of which was never invented down there!

His good-humour quite restored, Tartarin in a few sturdy strides struck the highroad to Fluelen, at the side of which the Hotel Tellsplatte spreads out its long facade. While awaiting the dinner-bell the guests were walking about in front of a cascade over rock-work on the gullied road, where landaus were drawn up, their poles on the ground among puddles of water in which was reflected a copper-coloured sun.

Tartarin inquired for his man. They told him he was dining. "Then take me to him, *zou!*" and this was said with such authority that in spite of the respectful repugnance shown to disturbing so important a personage, a maid-servant conducted the Alpinist through the whole hotel, where his advent created some amazement, to the invaluable courier who was dining alone in a little room that looked upon the court-yard.

"Monsieur," said Tartarin as he entered, his ice-axe on his shoulder, "excuse me if..."

He stopped stupefied, and the courier, tall, lank, his napkin at his chin, in the savoury steam of a plateful of hot soup, let fall his spoon.

"*Ve!* Monsieur Tartarin..."

"*Te!* Bompard."

It was Bompard, former manager of the Club, a good fellow, but afflicted with a fabulous imagination which rendered him incapable of telling a word of truth, and had caused him to be nicknamed in Tarascon "The Impostor."

Called an impostor in Tarascon! you can judge what he must have been. And this was the incomparable guide, the climber of the Alps, the Himalayas, the Mountains of the Moon.

"Oh! now, then, I understand," ejaculated Tartarin, rather nonplussed; but, even so, joyful to see a face from home and to hear once more that dear, delicious accent of the Cours.

"*Differemment*, Monsieur Tartarin, you 'll dine with me, *que?*"

Tartarin hastened to accept, delighted at the pleasure of sitting down at a private table opposite to a friend, without the very smallest litigious compote-dish between them, to be able to hobnob, to talk as he ate, and to eat good things, carefully cooked and fresh; for couriers are admirably treated by innkeepers, and served apart with all the best wines and the extra dainties.

Many were the *au mouains, pas mouains*, and *differemments*.

"Then, my dear fellow, it was really you I heard last night, up there, on the platform?.."

"Hey! *parfaitemain*... I was making those young ladies admire... Fine, isn't it, sunrise on the Alps?"

"Superb!" cried Tartarin, at first without conviction and merely to avoid contradicting him, but caught the next minute; and after that it was really bewildering to hear those two Tarasconese enthusiasts lauding the splendours they had found on the Rigi. It was Joanne capping Baedeker.

Then, as the meal went on, the conversation became more intimate, full of confidences and effusive protestations, which brought real tears to their Provencal eyes, lively, brilliant eyes, but keeping always in their facile emotion a little corner of jest and satire. In that alone did the two friends resemble each other; for in person one was as lean, tanned, weatherbeaten, seamed with the wrinkles special to the grimaces of his profession, as the other was short, stocky, sleek-skinned, and sound-blooded.

He had seen all, that poor Bompard, since his exodus from the Club. That insatiable imagination of his which prevented him from ever staying in one place had kept him wandering under so many suns, and through such diverse fortunes. He related his adventures, and counted up the fine occasions to enrich himself which had snapped, there! in his fingers--such as his last invention for saving the war-budget the cost of boots and shoes... "Do you know how?.. Oh, *moun Diou!* it is very simple... by shoeing the feet of the soldiers."

"*Outre!*" cried Tartarin, horrified.

Bompard continued very calmly, with his natural air of cold madness:--

"A great idea, wasn't it? Eh! *be!* at the ministry they did not even answer me... Ah! my poor Monsieur Tartarin, I have had my bad moments, I have eaten the bread of poverty before I entered the service of the Company..."

"Company! what Company?"

Bompard lowered his voice discreetly.

"Hush! presently, not here..." Then returning to his natural tones, "*Et autremain*, you people at Tarascon, what are you all doing? You haven't yet told me what brings you to our mountains..."

It was now for Tartarin to pour himself out. Without anger, but with that melancholy of declining years, that ennui which attacks as they grow elderly great artists, beautiful women, and all conquerors of peoples and hearts, he told of the defection of his compatriots, the plot laid against him to deprive him of the presidency, the decision he had come to to do some act of heroism, a great ascension, the Tarasconese banner borne higher than it had ever before been planted; in short, to prove to the Alpinists of Tarascon that he was still worthy... still worthy of... Emotion overcame him, he was forced to keep silence... Then he added:--

"You know me, Gonzague..." and nothing can ever render the effusion, the caressing charm with which he uttered that troubadouresque Christian name of the courier. It was like one way of pressing his hands, of coming nearer to his heart... "You know me, *que!* You know if I balked when the question came up of marching upon the lion; and during the war, when we organized together the defences of the Club..."

Bompard nodded his head with terrible emphasis; he thought he was there still.

"Well, my good fellow, what the lions, what the Krupp cannon could never do, the Alps have accomplished... I am afraid."

"Don't say that, Tartarin!"

"Why not?" said the hero, with great gentleness... "I say it, because it is so..."

And tranquilly, without posing, he acknowledged the impression made upon him by Dore's drawing of that catastrophe on the Matterhorn, which was ever before his eyes. He feared those perils, and being told of an extraordinary guide, capable of avoiding them, he resolved to seek him out and confide in him.

Then, in a tone more natural, he added: "You have never been a guide, have you, Gonzague?"

"*He!* yes," replied Bompard, smiling... "Only, I never did all that I related."

"That's understood," assented Tartarin.

And the other added in a whisper:--

"Let us go out on the road; we can talk more freely there."

It was getting dark; a warm damp breeze was rolling up black clouds upon the sky, where the setting sun had left behind it a vague gray mist.

They went along the shore in the direction of Fluelen, crossing the mute shadows of hungry tourists returning to the hotel; shadows themselves, and not speaking until they reached a tunnel through which the road is cut, opening at intervals to little terraces overhanging the lake.

"Let us stop here," pealed forth the hollow voice of Bompard, which resounded under the vaulted roof like a cannon-shot. There, seated on the parapet, they con-templated that admirable view of the lake, the downward rush of the fir-trees and beeches pressing blackly together in the foreground, and farther on, the higher mountains with waving summits, and farther still, others of a bluish-gray confusion as of clouds, in the midst of which lay, though scarcely visible, the long white trail of a glacier, winding through the hollows and suddenly illumined with irised fire, yellow, red, and green. They were exhibiting the mountain with Bengal lights!

From Fluelen the rockets rose, scattering their multicoloured stars; Venetian lanterns went and came in boats that remained invisible while bearing bands of music and pleasure-seekers.

A fairylike decoration seen through the frame, cold and architectural, of the granite walls of the tunnel.

"What a queer country, **pas mouain**, this Switzerland..." cried Tartarin.

Bompard burst out laughing.

"Ah! **vai**, Switzerland!.. In the first place, there is no Switzerland."

V.

Confidences in a tunnel.

"Switzerland, in our day, **ve!** Monsieur Tar-tarin, is nothing more than a vast Kursaal, open from June to September, a panoramic casino, where people come from all four quarters of the globe to amuse themselves, and which is manipulated and managed by a Company **richissime** by hundreds of thousands of millions, which has its offices in London and Geneva. It costs money, you may be sure, to lease and brush up and trick out all this territory, lakes, forests, mountains, cascades, and to keep a whole people of employes, supernumeraries, and what not, and set up mi-raculous hotels on the highest summits, with gas, telegraphs, telephones..."

"That, at least, is true," said Tartarin, thinking aloud, and remembering the Rigi.

"True!.. But you have seen nothing yet... Go on through the country and you 'll not find one corner that is n't engineered and machine-worked like the under stage of the Opera,--cascades lighted *a giorno*, turnstiles at the entrance to the glaciers, and loads of railways, hydraulic and funicular, for ascensions. To be sure, the Company, in view of its clients the English and American climbers, keeps up on the noted mountains, Jungfrau, Monk, Finsteraarhorn, an appearance of danger and desolation, though in reality there is no more risk there than elsewhere..."

"But the crevasses, my good fellow, those horrible crevasses... Suppose one falls into them?"

"You fall on snow, Monsieur Tartarin, and you don't hurt yourself, and there is always at the bottom a porter, a hunter, at any rate some one, who picks you up, shakes and brushes you, and asks graciously: 'Has monsieur any baggage?'"

"What stuff are you telling me now, Gonzague?"

Bompard redoubled in gravity.

"The keeping up of those crevasses is one of the heaviest expenses of the Company."

Silence fell for a moment under the tunnel, the surroundings of which were quieting down. No more varied fireworks, Bengal lights, or boats on the water; but the moon had risen and made another conventional landscape, bluish, liquidescent, with masses of impenetrable shadow...

Tartarin hesitated to believe his companion on his word. Nevertheless, he reflected on the extraordinary things he had seen in four days--the sun on the Rigi, the farce of William Tell--and Bompard's inventions seemed to him all the more probable because in every Tarasconese the braggart is leashed with a gull.

"*Differemment*, my good friend, how do you explain certain awful catastrophes... that of the Matterhorn, for instance?.."

"It is sixteen years since that happened; the Company was not then constituted, Monsieur Tartarin."

"But last year, the accident on the Wetterhorn, two guides buried with their travellers!.."

"Must, sometimes, *te, pardi!*.. you understand... whets the Alpinists... The English won't come to mountains now where heads are not broke... The Wetterhorn had been running down for some time, but after that little item in the papers the receipts went up at once."

"Then the two guides?.."

"They are just as safe as the travellers; only they are kept out of sight, supported in foreign parts, for six months... A puff like that costs dear, but the Company is rich enough to afford it."

"Listen to me, Gonzague..."

Tartarin had risen, one hand on Bompard's shoulder.

"You would not wish to have any misfortune happen to me, *que?*.. Well, then! speak to me frankly... you know my capacities as an Alpinist; they are moderate."

"Very moderate, that's true."

"Do you think, nevertheless, that I could, without too much danger, undertake the ascension of the Jungfrau?"

"I 'll answer for it, my head in the fire, Monsieur Tartarin... You have only to trust to your guide, *ve!*"

"And if I turn giddy?"

"Shut your eyes."

"And if I slip?"

"Let yourself go... just as they do on the stage... sort of trap-doors... there 's no risk..."

"Ah! if I could have you there to tell me all that, to keep repeating it to me... Look here, my good fellow, make an effort, and come with me."

Bompard desired nothing better, *pecaire!* but he had those Peruvians on his hands for the rest of the season; and, replying to his old friend, who expressed surprise at seeing him accept the functions of a courier, a subaltern,--

"I could n't help myself, Monsieur Tartarin," he said. "It is in our engagement. The Company has the right to employ us as it pleases."

On which he began to count upon his fingers his varied avatars during the last three years... guide in the Oberland, performer on the Alpine horn, chamois-hunter, veteran soldier of Charles X., Protestant pastor on the heights...

"*Ques aco?*" demanded Tartarin, astonished.

"*Be!* yes," replied the other, composedly. "When you travel in German Switzerland you will see pastors preaching on giddy heights, standing on rocks or rustic pulpits of the trunks of trees. A few shepherds and cheese-makers, their leather caps in their hands, and women with their heads dressed up in the costume of the canton group themselves about in picturesque attitudes; the scenery is pretty, the pastures green, or the harvest just over, cascades to the road, and flocks with their bells ringing every note on the mountain. All that, *ve* that's decorative, suggestive. Only, none but the employes of the Company, guides, pastors, couriers, hotel-keepers are in the secret, and it is their interest not to let it get wind, for fear of startling the clients."

The Alpinist was dumfounded, silent--in him the acme of stupefaction. In his heart, whatever doubt he may have had as to Bompard's veracity, he felt himself comforted and calmed as to Alpine ascensions, and presently the conversation grew joyous. The two friends talked of Tarascon, of their good, hearty laughs in the olden time when both were younger.

"Apropos of *galejade* [jokes]," said Tartarin, suddenly, "they played me a fine one on the Rigi-Kulm... Just imagine that this morning..." and he told of the letter gummed to his glass, reciting it with emphasis: "'Devil of a Frenchman'... A hoax, of course, *que?*"

"May be... who knows?.." said Bompard, seeming to take the matter more seriously. He asked if Tartarin during his stay on the Rigi had relations with any one, and whether he had n't said a word too much.

"Ha! *vai!* a word too much! as if one even opened one's mouth among those English and Germans, mute as carp under pretence of good manners!"

On reflection, however, he did remember having clinched a matter, and sharply too! with a species of Cossack, a certain Mi... Milanof.

"Manilof," corrected Bompard.

"Do you know him?.. Between you and me, I think that Manilof had a spite against me about a little Russian girl..."

"Yes, Sonia... "murmured Bompard.

"Do you know her too? Ah! my friend, a pearl! a pretty little gray partridge!"

"Sonia Wassilief... It was she who killed with one shot of her revolver in the open that General Felianine, the president of the Council of War which condemned her brother to perpetual exile."

Sonia an assassin? that child, that little blond fairy!.. Tartarin could not believe it. But Bompard gave precise particulars and details of the affair--which, indeed, is very well known. Sonia had lived for the last two years in Zurich, where her brother Boris, having escaped from Siberia, joined her, his lungs gone; and during the summers she took him for better air to the mountains. Bompard had often met them, attended by friends who were all exiles, conspirators. The Wassiliefs, very intelligent, very energetic, and still possessed of some fortune, were at the head of the Nihilist party, with Bolibine, the man who murdered the prefect of police, and this very Manilof, who blew up the Winter Palace last year.

"*Boufre!*" exclaimed Tartarin, "one meets with queer neighbours on the Rigi."

But here's another thing. Bompard took it into his head that Tartarin's letter came from these young people; it was just like their Nihilist proceedings. The czar, every morning, found warnings in his study, under his napkin...

"But," said Tartarin, turning pale, "why such threats? What have I done to them?"

Bompard thought they must have taken him for a spy.

"A spy! I!

"*Be!* yes." In all the Nihilist centres, at Zurich, Lausanne, Geneva, Russia maintained at great cost, a numerous body of spies; in fact, for some time past she had had in her service the former chief of the French Imperial police, with a dozen Corsicans, who followed and watched all Russian exiles, and took countless disguises in order to detect them. The costume of the Alpinist, his spectacles, his accent, were quite enough to confound him in their minds with those agents.

"*Coquin de sort!* now I think of it," said Tartarin, "they had at their heels the whole time a rascally Italian tenor... undoubtedly a spy... *Differemment*, what must I do?"

"Above all things, never put yourself in the way of those people again; now that they have warned you they will do you harm..."

"Ha! *vai! harm!*.. The first one that comes near me I shall cleave his head with my ice-axe."

And in the gloom of the tunnel the eyes of the Tarasconese hero glared. But Bompard, less confident than he, knew well that the hatred of Nihilists is terrible; it attacks from below, it undermines, and plots. It is all very well to be a *lapin* like the president, but you had better beware of that inn bed you sleep in, and the chair you sit upon, and the rail of the steamboat, which will give way suddenly and drop you to death. And think of the cooking-dishes prepared, the glass rubbed over with invisible poison!

"Beware of the kirsch in your flask, and the frothing milk that cow-man in sabots brings you. They stop at nothing, I tell you."

"If so, what's to be done! I'm doomed!" groaned Tartarin; then, grasping the hand of his companion:--

"Advise me, Gonzague."

After a moment's reflection, Bompard traced out to him a programme. To leave the next day, early, cross the lake and the Bruenig pass, and sleep at Interlaken. The next day, to Grindelwald and the Little Scheideck. And the day after, the JUNG-FRAU! After that, home to Tarascon, without losing an hour, or looking back.

"I 'll start to-morrow, Gonzague..." declared the hero, in a virile voice, with a look of terror at the mysterious horizon, now dim in the darkness, and at the lake which seemed to him to harbour all treachery beneath the glassy calm of its pale reflections.

VI.

The Bruenig pass. Tartarin falls into the hands of Nihilists,
Disappearance of an Italian tenor and a rope made at
Avignon, Fresh exploits of the cap-sportsman. Pan! pan!

"Get in! get in!"

"But how the devil, que! am I to get in? the places are full... they won't make room for me."

This was said at the extreme end of the lake of the Four Cantons, on that shore at Alpnach, damp and soggy as a delta, where the post-carriages wait in line to convey tourists leaving the boat to cross the Bruenig.

A fine rain like needle-points had been falling since morning; and the worthy Tartarin, hampered by his armament, hustled by the porters and the custom-house officials, ran from carriage to carriage, sonorous and lumbering as that orchestra-man one sees at fairs, whose every movement sets a-going triangles, big drums,

Chinese bells, and cymbals. At all the doors the same cry of terror, the same crabbed "Full!" growled in all dialects, the same swelling-out of bodies and garments to take as much room as possible and prevent the entrance of so dangerous and resounding a companion.

The unfortunate Alpinist puffed, sweated, and replied with "***Coquin de bon sort!***" and despairing gestures to the impatient clamour of the convoy: "En route!.. All right!.. Andiamo!.. Vorwarts!.." The horses pawed, the drivers swore. Finally, the manager of the post-route, a tall, ruddy fellow in a tunic and flat cap, interfered himself, and opening forcibly the door of a landau, the top of which was half up, he pushed in Tartarin, hoisting him like a bundle, and then stood, majestically, with outstretched hand for his *trinkgeld*.

Humiliated, furious with the people in the carriage who were forced to accept him *manu militari*, Tartarin affected not to look at them, rammed his porte-monnaie back into his pocket, wedged his ice-axe on one side of him with ill-humoured motions and an air of determined brutality, as if he were a passenger by the Dover steamer landing at Calais.

"Good-morning, monsieur," said a gentle voice he had heard already.

He raised his eyes, and sat horrified, terrified before the pretty, round and rosy face of Sonia, seated directly in front of him, beneath the hood of the landau, which also sheltered a tall young man, wrapped in shawls and rugs, of whom nothing could be seen but a forehead of livid paleness and a few thin meshes of hair, golden like the rim of his near-sighted spectacles. A third person, whom Tartarin knew but too well, accompanied them,--Manilof, the incendiary of the Winter Palace.

Sonia, Manilof, what a mouse-trap!

This was the moment when they meant to accomplish their threat, on that Bruenig pass, so craggy, so surrounded with abysses. And the hero, by one of those flashes of horror which reveal the depths of danger, beheld himself stretched on the rocks of a ravine, or swinging from the topmost branches of an oak. Fly! yes, but where, how? The vehicles had started in file at the sound of a trumpet, a crowd of little ragamuffins were clambering at the doors with bunches of edelweiss. Tartarin, maddened, had a mind to begin the attack by cleaving the head of the Cossack beside him with his alpenstock; then, on reflection, he felt it was more prudent to refrain. Evidently, these people would not attempt their scheme till farther on, in regions uninhabited, and before that, there might come means of getting out. Besides, their intentions no longer seemed to him quite so malevolent. Sonia smiled gently upon him from her pretty turquoise eyes, the pale young man looked pleasantly at him, and Manilof, visibly milder, moved obligingly aside and helped him to put his bag between them. Had they discovered their mistake by reading on the register of the Rigi-Kulm the illustrious name of Tartarin?.. He wished to make sure, and, familiarly, good-humouredly, he began:--

"Enchanted with this meeting, beautiful young lady... only, permit me to introduce myself... you are ignorant with whom you have to do, *ve!* whereas, I am perfectly aware who *you* are."

"Hush!" said the little Sonia, still smiling, but pointing with her gloved finger to the seat beside the driver, where sat the tenor with his sleeve-buttons, and another young Russian, sheltering themselves under the same umbrella, and laughing and talking in Italian.

Between the police and the Nihilists, Tartarin did not hesitate.

"Do you know that man, *au mouain?*" he said in a low voice, putting his head quite close to Sonia's fresh cheeks, and seeing himself in her clear eyes, which suddenly turned hard and savage as she answered "yes," with a snap of their lids.

The hero shuddered, but as one shudders at the theatre, with that delightful creeping of the epidermis which takes you when the action becomes Corsican, and you settle yourself in your seat to see and to listen more attentively. Personally out of the affair, delivered from the mortal terrors which had haunted him all night and prevented him from swallowing his usual Swiss coffee, honey, and butter, he breathed with free lungs, thought life good, and this little Russian irresistibly pleasing in her travelling hat, her jersey close to the throat, tight to the arms, and moulding her slender figure of perfect elegance. And such a child! Child in the candour of her laugh, in the down upon her cheeks, in the pretty grace with which she spread her shawl upon the knees of her poor brother. "Are you comfortable?.." "You are not cold?" How could any one suppose that little hand, so delicate beneath its chamois glove, had had the physical force and the moral courage to kill a man?

Nor did the others of the party seem ferocious: all had the same ingenuous laugh, rather constrained and sad on the drawn lips of the poor invalid, and noisy in Manilof, who, very young behind his bushy beard, gave way to explosions of mirth like a schoolboy in his holidays, bursts of a gayety that was really exuberant.

The third companion, whom they called Boli-bine, and who talked on the box with the tenor, amused himself much and was constantly turning back to translate to his friends the Italian's adventures, his successes at the Petersburg Opera, his **bonnes fortunes**, the sleeve-buttons the ladies had subscribed to present to him on his departure, extraordinary buttons, with, three notes of music engraved thereon, *la do re* (l'adore), which professional pun, repeated in the landau, caused such delight, the tenor himself swelling up with pride and twirling his moustache with so silly and conquering a look at Sonia, that Tartarin began to ask himself whether, after all, they were not mere tourists, and he a genuine tenor.

Meantime the carriages, going at a good pace, rolled over bridges, skirted little lakes and flowery meads, and fine vineyards running with water and deserted; for it was Sunday, and all the peasants whom they met wore their gala costumes, the women with long braids of hair hanging down their backs and silver chainlets. They began at last to mount the road in zigzags among forests of oak and beech; little by little the marvellous horizon displayed itself on the left; at each turn of the zigzag, rivers, valleys with their spires pointing upward came into view, and far away in the distance, the hoary head of the Finsteraarhorn, whitening beneath an invisible sun.

Soon the road became gloomy, the aspect savage. On one side, heavy shadows, a chaos of trees, twisted and gnarled on a steep slope, down which foamed a torrent noisily; to right, an enormous rock overhanging the road and bristling with branches that sprouted from its fissures.

They laughed no more in the landau; but they all admired, raising their heads and trying to see the summit of this tunnel of granite.

"The forests of Atlas!.. I seem to see them again..." said Tartarin, gravely, and then, as the remark passed unnoticed, he added: "Without the lion's roar, however."

"You have heard it, monsieur?" asked Sonia.

Heard the lion, he!.. Then, with an indulgent smile: "I am Tartarin of Tarascon, mademoiselle..."

And just see what such barbarians are! He might have said, "My name is Dupont;" it would have been exactly the same thing to them. They were ignorant of the name of Tartarin!

Nevertheless, he was not angry, and he answered the young lady, who wished to know if the lion's roar had frightened him: "No, mademoiselle... My camel trembled between my legs, but I looked to my priming as tranquilly as before a herd of cows... At a distance their cry is much the same, like this, *te!*"

To give Sonia an exact impression of the thing, he bellowed in his most sonorous voice a formidable "Meuh..." which swelled, spread, echoed and reechoed against the rock. The horses reared; in all the carriages the travellers sprang up alarmed, looking round for the accident, the cause of such an uproar; but recognizing the Alpinist, whose head and overwhelming accoutrements could be seen in the uncovered half of the landau, they asked themselves once more: "Who is that animal?"

He, very calm, continued to give details: when to attack the beast, where to strike him, how to despatch him, and about the diamond sight he affixed to his carbines to enable him to aim correctly in the darkness. The young girl listened to him, leaning forward with a little panting of the nostrils, in deep attention.

"They say that Bombonnel still hunts; do you know him?" asked the brother.

"Yes," replied Tartarin, without enthusiasm... "He is not a clumsy fellow, but we have better than he."

A word to the wise! Then in a melancholy tone, "*Pas mouain*, they give us strong emotions, these hunts of the great carnivora. When we have them no longer life seems empty; we do not know how to fill it."

Here Manilof, who understood French without speaking it, and seemed to be listening to Tartarin very intently, his peasant forehead slashed with the wrinkle of a great scar, said a few words, laughing, to his friends.

"Manilof says we are all of the same brotherhood," explained Sonia to Tartarin... "We hunt, like you, the great wild beasts."

"*Te!* yes, *pardi*... wolves, white bears..."

"Yes, wolves, white bears, and other noxious animals..."

And the laughing began again, noisy, interminable, but in a sharp, ferocious key this time, laughs that showed their teeth and reminded Tartarin in what sad and singular company he was travelling.

Suddenly the carriages stopped. The road became steeper and made at this spot a long circuit to reach the top of the Bruenig pass, which could also be reached on foot in twenty minutes less time through a noble forest of birches. In spite of the rain in the morning, making the earth sodden and slippery, the tourists nearly all left the carriages and started, single file, along the narrow path called a *schlittage*.

From Tartarin's landau, the last in line, all the men got out; but Sonia, thinking the path too muddy, settled herself back in the carriage, and as the Alpinist was getting out with the rest, a little delayed by his equipments, she said to him in a low voice: "Stay! keep me company..." in such a coaxing way! The poor man, quite overcome, began immediately to forge a romance, as delightful as it was improbable, which made his old heart beat and throb.

He was quickly undeceived when he saw the young girl leaning anxiously forward to watch Bolibine and the Italian, who were talking eagerly together at the opening of the path, Manilof and Boris having already gone forward. The so-called tenor hesitated. An instinct seemed to warn him not to risk himself alone in company with those three men. He decided at last to go on, and Sonia looked at him as he mounted the path, all the while stroking her cheek with a bouquet of purple cyclamen, those mountain violets, the leaf of which is lined with the same fresh colour as the flowers.

The landau proceeded slowly. The driver got down to walk in front with other comrades, and the convoy of more than fifteen empty vehicles, drawn nearer together by the steepness of the road, rolled silently along. Tartarin, greatly agitated, and foreboding something sinister, dared not look at his companion, so much did he fear that a word or a look might compel him to be an actor in the drama he felt impending. But Sonia was paying no attention to him; her eyes were rather fixed, and she did not cease caressing the down of her skin mechanically with the flowers.

"So," she said at length, "so you know who we are, I and my friends... Well, what do you think of us? What do Frenchmen think of us?"

The hero turned pale, then red. He was desirous of not offending by rash or imprudent words such vindictive beings; on the other hand, how consort with murderers? He got out of it by a metaphor:--

"*Differemment*, mademoiselle, you were telling me just now that we belonged to the same brotherhood, hunters of hydras and monsters, despots and carnivora... It is therefore to a companion of St. Hubert that I now make answer... My sentiment is that, even against wild beasts we should use loyal weapons... Our Jules Gerard, a famous lion-slayer, employed explosive balls. I myself have never given in to that, I do not use them... When I hunted the lion or the panther I planted myself before the beast, face to face, with a good double-barrelled carbine, and pan! pan! a ball in each eye."

"In each eye!.." repeated Sonia.

"Never did I miss my aim."

He affirmed it and he believed it.

The young girl looked at him with naive admiration, thinking aloud:--

"That must certainly be the surest way."

A sudden rending of the branches and the underbrush, and the thicket parted above them, so quickly and in so feline a way that Tartarin, his head now full of hunting adventures, might have thought himself still on the watch in the Zaccar. But Manilof sprang from the slope, noiselessly, and close to the carriage. His small, cunning eyes were shining in a face that was flayed by the briers; his beard and his long lank hair were streaming with water from the branches. Breathless, holding with his coarse, hairy hands to the doorway, he spoke in Russian to Sonia, who turned instantly to Tartarin and said in a curt voice:--

"Your rope... quick..."

"My... my rope?.." stammered the hero.

"Quick, quick... you shall have it again in half an hour."

Offering no other explanation, she helped him with her little gloved hands to divest himself of his famous rope made in Avignon. Manilof took the coil, grunting with joy; in two bounds he sprang, with the elasticity of a wild-cat, into the thicket and disappeared.

"What has happened? What are they going to do?.. He looked ferocious..." murmured Tartaric not daring to utter his whole thought.

Ferocious, Manilof! Ah! how plain it was he did not know him. No human being was ever better, gentler, more compassionate; and to show Tartarin a trait of that exceptionally kind nature, Sonia, with her clear, blue glance, told him how her friend, having executed a dangerous mandate of the Revolutionary Committee and jumped into the sledge which awaited him for escape, had threatened the driver to get out, cost what it might, if he persisted in whipping the horse whose fleetness alone could save him.

Tartarin thought the act worthy of antiquity. Then, having reflected on all the human lives sacrificed by that same Manilof, as conscienceless as an earthquake or a volcano in eruption, who yet would not let others hurt an animal in his presence, he questioned the young girl with an ingenuous air:--

"Were there many killed by the explosion at the Winter Palace?"

"Too many," replied Sonia, sadly; "and the only one that ought to have died escaped."

She remained silent, as if displeased, looking so pretty, her head lowered, with her long auburn eyelashes sweeping her pale rose cheeks. Tartarin, angry with himself for having pained her, was caught once more by that charm of youth and freshness which the strange little creature shed around her.

"So, monsieur, the war that we are making seems to you unjust, inhuman?" She said it quite close to him in a caress, as it were, of her breath and her eye; the hero felt himself weakening...

"You do not see that all means are good and legitimate to deliver a people who groan and suffocate?.."

"No doubt, no doubt..."

The young girl, growing more insistent as Tartarin weakened, went on:--

"You spoke just now of a void to be filled; does it not seem to you more noble, more interesting to risk your life for a great cause than to risk it in slaying lions or scaling glaciers?"

"The fact is," said Tartarin, intoxicated, losing his head and mad with an irresistible desire to take and kiss that ardent, persuasive little hand which she laid upon his arm, as she had done once before, up there, on the Rigi when he put on her shoe. Finally, unable to resist, and seizing the little gloved hand between both his own,--

"Listen, Sonia," he said, in a good hearty voice, paternal and familiar... "Listen, Sonia..."

A sudden stop of the landau interrupted him. They had reached the summit of the Bruenig; travellers and drivers were getting into their carriages to catch up lost time and reach, at a gallop, the next village where the convoy was to breakfast and relay. The three Russians took their places, but that of the Italian tenor remained unoccupied.

"That gentleman got into one of the first carriages," said Boris to the driver, who asked about him; then, addressing Tartarin, whose uneasiness was visible:--

"We must ask him for your rope; he chose to keep it with him."

Thereupon, fresh laughter in the landau, and the resumption for poor Tartarin of horrid perplexity, not knowing what to think or believe in presence of the good-humour and ingenuous countenances of the suspected assassins. Sonia, while wrapping up her invalid in cloaks and plaids, for the air on the summit was all the keener from the rapidity with which the carriages were now driven, related in Russian her conversation with Tartarin, uttering his pan! pan! with a pretty intonation which her companions repeated after her, two of them admiring the hero, while Manilof shook his head incredulously.

The relay!

This was on the market-place of a large village, at an old tavern with a worm-eaten wooden balcony, and a sign hanging to a rusty iron bracket. The file of vehicles stopped, and while the horses were being unharnessed the hungry tourists jumped hurriedly down and rushed into a room on the lower floor, painted green and smelling of mildew, where the table was laid for twenty guests. Sixty had arrived, and for five minutes nothing could be heard but a frightful tumult, cries, and a vehement altercation between the Rices and the Prunes around the compote-dishes, to the great alarm of the tavern-keeper, who lost his head (as if daily, at the same hour, the same post-carriages did not pass) and bustled about his servants, also seized with chronic bewilderment--excellent method of serving only half the dishes called for by the *carte*, and of giving change in a way that made the white sous of Switzerland count for fifty centimes. "Suppose we dine in the carriage," said Sonia, I annoyed by such confusion; and as no one had time to pay attention to them the young men themselves did the waiting. Manilof returned with a cold leg of mutton, Bolibine with a long loaf of bread and sausages; but the best forager was Tartarin. Certainly the opportunity to get away from his companions in the bustle of relay ing was a fine one; he might at least have assured himself that the Italian had reappeared; but he never once thought of it, being solely preoccupied with Sonia's breakfast, and in showing Manilof and the others how a Tarasconese can manage matters.

When he stepped down the portico of the hotel, gravely, with fixed eyes, bearing in his robust hands a large tray laden with plates, napkins, assorted food, and Swiss champagne in its gilt-necked bottles, Sonia clapped her hands, and congratulated him.

"How did you manage it?" she said.

"I don't know... somehow, *te!*.. We are all like that in Tarascon."

Oh! those happy minutes! That pleasant breakfast opposite to Sonia, almost on his knees, the village market-place, like the scene of an operetta, with clumps of green trees, beneath which sparkled the gold ornaments and the muslin sleeves of the Swiss girls, walking about, two and two, like dolls!

How good the bread tasted! what savoury sausages! The heavens themselves took part in the scene, and were soft, veiled, clement; it rained, of course, but so gently, the drops so rare, though just enough to temper the Swiss champagne, always dangerous to Southern heads.

Under the veranda of the hotel, a Tyrolian quartette, two giants and two female dwarfs in resplendent and heavy rags, looking as if they had escaped from the failure of a theatre at a fair, were mingling their throat notes: "aou... aou..." with the clinking of plates and glasses. They were ugly, stupid, motionless, straining the cords of their skinny necks. Tartarin thought them delightful, and gave them a handful of sous, to the great amazement of the villagers who surrounded the un-horsed landau.

"Vife la Vranze!" quavered a voice in the crowd, from which issued a tall old man, clothed in a singular blue coat with silver buttons, the skirts of which swept the ground; on his head was a gigantic shako, in form like a bucket of sauerkraut, and so weighted by its enormous plume that the old man was forced to balance himself with his arms as he walked, like an acrobat.

"Old soldier... Charles X..."

Tartarin, fresh from Bompard's revelations, began to laugh, and said in a low voice with a wink of his eye:--

"Up to *that*, old fellow..." But even so, he gave him a white sou and poured him out a bumper, which the old man accepted, laughing, and winking himself, though without knowing why. Then, dislodging from a corner of his mouth an enormous china pipe, he raised his glass and drank "to the company," which confirmed Tartarin in his opinion that here was a colleague of Bompard.

No matter! one toast deserved another. So, standing up in the carriage, his glass held high, his voice strong, Tartarin brought tears to his eyes by drinking, first: To France, my country!.. next to hospitable Switzerland, which he was happy to honour publicly and thank for the generous welcome she affords to the vanquished, to the exiled of all lands. Then, lowering his voice and inclining his glass to the companions of his journey, he wished them a quick return to their country, restoration to their family, safe friends, honourable careers, and an end to all dissensions; for, he said, it is impossible to spend one's life in eating each other up.

During the utterance of this toast Soma's brother smiled, cold and sarcastic behind his blue spectacles; Manilof, his neck pushed forth, his swollen eyebrows emphasizing his wrinkle, seemed to be asking himself if that "big barrel" would soon be done with his gabble, while Bolibine, perched on the box, was twisting his comical yellow face, wrinkled as a Barbary ape, till he looked like one of those villanous little monkeys squatting on the shoulders of the Alpinist.

The young girl alone listened to him very seriously, striving to comprehend such a singular type of man. Did he think all that he said? Had he done all that he related? Was he a madman, a comedian, or simply a gabbler, as Manilof in his quality of man of action insisted, giving to the word a most contemptuous signification.

The answer was given at once. His toast ended, Tartarin had just sat down when a sudden shot, a second, then a third, fired close to the tavern, brought him again to his feet, ears straining and nostrils scenting powder.

"Who fired?.. where is it?.. what is happening?.."

In his inventive noddle a whole drama was already defiling; attack on the convoy by armed bands; opportunity given him to defend the honour and life of that charming young lady. But no! the discharges only came from the Stand, where the youths of the village practise at a mark every Sunday. As the horses were not yet harnessed, Tartarin, as if carelessly, proposed to go and look at them. He had his idea, and Sonia had hers in accepting the proposal. Guided by the old soldier of Charles X. wobbling under his shako, they crossed the market-place, opening the ranks of the crowd, who followed them with curiosity.

Beneath its thatched roof and its square uprights of pine wood the Stand resembled one of our own pistol-galleries at a fair, with this difference, that the amateurs brought their own weapons, breech-loading muskets of the oldest pattern, which they managed, however, with some adroitness. Tar-tarin, his arms crossed, observed the shots, criticised them aloud, gave his advice, but did not fire himself. The Russians watched him, making signs to each other.

"Pan!.. pan!.." sneered Bolibine, making the gesture of taking aim and mimicking Tartarin's accent. Tartarin turned round very red, and swelling with anger.

"*Parfaitemain*, young man... Pan!.. pan!.. and as often as you like."

The time to load an old double-barrelled carbine which must have served several generations of chamois hunters, and--pan!.. pan!.. T is done. Both balls are in the bull's-eye. Hurrahs of admiration burst forth on all sides. Sonia triumphed. Bolibine laughed no more.

"But that is nothing, that!" said Tartarin; "you shall see..."

The Stand did not suffice him; he looked about for another target, and the crowd recoiled alarmed from this strange Alpinist, thick-set, savage-looking and carbine in hand, when they heard him propose to the old guard of Charles X. to break his pipe between his teeth at fifty paces. The old fellow howled in terror and plunged into the crowd, his trembling plume remaining visible above their serried heads. None the less, Tartarin felt that he must put it somewhere, that ball. "*Te! pardi!* as we did at Tarascon!.." And the former cap-hunter pitched his headgear high into the air with all the strength of his double muscles, shot it on the fly, and pierced it. "Bravo!" cried Sonia, sticking into the small hole made by the ball the bouquet of cyclamen with which she had stroked her cheek.

With that charming trophy in his cap Tartarin returned to the landau. The trumpet sounded, the convoy started, the horses went rapidly down to Brienz along that marvellous corniche road, blasted in the side of the rock, separated from an abyss of over a thousand feet by single stones a couple of yards apart. But Tartarin was no longer conscious of danger; no longer did he look at the scenery--that Meyringen valley, seen through a light veil of mist, with its river in straight lines, the lake, the villages massing themselves in the distance, and that whole horizon of mountains, of glaciers, blending at times with the clouds, displaced by the turns of the road, lost apparently, and then returning, like the shifting scenes of a stage.

Softened by tender thoughts, the hero admired the sweet child before him, reflecting that glory is only a semi-happiness, that 'tis sad to grow old all alone in your greatness, like Moses, and that this fragile flower of the North transplanted into the little garden at Tarascon would brighten its monotony, and be sweeter to see and breathe than that everlasting baobab, ***arbos gigantea***, diminutively confined in the mignonette pot. With her childlike eyes, and her broad brow, thoughtful and self-willed, Sonia looked at him, and she, too, dreamed--but who knows what the young girls dream of?

VII.

The nights at Tarascon, Where is he? Anxiety. The
grasshoppers on the promenade call for Tartarin. Martyrdom
of a great Tarasconese saint. The Club of the Alpines. What
was happening at the pharmacy. "Help! help! Bezuquet!"

"A letter, Monsieur Bezuquet!.. Comes from Switzerland, ***vé!*.. Switzerland!" cried the postman joyously, from the other end of the little square, waving something in the air, and hurrying along in the coming darkness.

The apothecary, who took the air, as they say, of an evening before his door in his shirt-sleeves, gave a jump, seized the letter with feverish hands and carried it into his lair among the varied odours of elixirs and dried herbs, but did not open it till the postman had departed, refreshed by a glass of that delicious ***sirop de cadavre*** in recompense for what he brought.

Fifteen days had Bezuquet expected it, this letter from Switzerland, fifteen days of agonized watching! And here it was. Merely from looking at the cramped and resolute little writing on the envelope, the postmark "Interlaken" and the broad purple stamp of the "Hotel Jungfrau, kept by Meyer," the tears filled his eyes, and the heavy moustache of the Barbary corsair through which whispered softly the idle whistle of a kindly soul, quivered.

"***Confidential. Destroy when read.***" Those words, written large at the head of the page, in the telegraphic style of the pharmacopoeia ("external use; shake before using") troubled him to the point of making him read aloud, as one does in a bad dream: "***Fearful things are happening to me***..." In the salon beside the pharmacy where she was taking her little nap after supper, Mme. Bezuquet, **mere**, might hear him, or the pupil whose pestle was pounding its regular blows in the big marble mortar of the laboratory. Bezuquet continued his reading in a low voice, beginning it over again two or three times, very pale, his hair literally standing on end. Then, with a rapid look about him, **cra cra**... and the letter in a thousand scraps went into the waste-paper basket; but there it might be found, and pieced together, and as he was stooping to gather up the fragments a quavering voice called to him:

"**Ve!** Ferdinand, are you there?" "Yes, mamma," replied the unlucky corsair, curdling with fear, the whole of his long body on its hands and knees beneath the desk. "What are you doing, my treasure?" "I am... h'm, I am making Mile. Tourna-toire's eye-salve."

Mamma went to sleep again, the pupil's pestle, suspended for a moment, began once more its slow clock movement, while Bezuquet walked up and down before his door in the deserted little square, turning pink or green according as he passed before one or other of his bottles. From time to time he threw up his arms, uttering disjointed words: "Unhappy man!.. lost... fatal love... how can we extricate him?" and, in spite of his trouble of mind, accompanying with a lively whistle the bugle "taps" of a dragoon regiment echoing among the plane-trees of the Tour de Ville.

"**He!** good night, Bezuquet," said a shadow hurrying along in the ash-coloured twilight.

"Where are you going, Pegoulade?"

"To the Club, **pardi!**.. Night session... they are going to discuss Tartarin and the presidency... You ought to come."

"**Te!** yes, I 'll come..." said the apothecary vehemently, a providential idea darting through his mind. He went in, put on his frock-coat, felt in its pocket to assure himself that his latchkey was there, and also the American tomahawk, without which no Tarasconese whatsoever would risk himself in the streets after "taps." Then he called: "Pascalon!.. Pascalon!.." but not too loudly, for fear of waking the old lady.

Almost a child, though bald, wearing all his hair in his curly blond beard, Pas-calon the pupil had the ardent soul of a partizan, a dome-like forehead, the eyes of crazy goat, and on his chubby cheeks the delicate tints of a shiny crusty Beaucaire roll. On all the grand Alpine excursions it was to him that the Club entrusted its banner, and his childish soul had vowed to the P. C. A. a fanatical worship, the burning, silent adoration of a taper consuming itself before an altar in the Easter season.

"Pascalon," said the apothecary in a low voice, and so close to him that the bristle of his moustache pricked his ear. "I have news of Tartarin... It is heart-breaking..."

Seeing him turn pale, he added:

"Courage, child! all can be repaired... ***Differemment*** I confide to you the pharmacy... If any one asks you for arsenic, don't give it; opium, don't give that either, nor rhubarb... don't give anything. If I am not in by ten o'clock, lock the door and go to bed."

With intrepid step, he plunged into the darkness, not once looking back, which allowed Pascalon to spring at the waste-paper basket, turn it over and over with feverish eager hands and finally tip out its contents on the leather of the desk to see if no scrap remained of the mysterious letter brought by the postman.

To those who know Tarasconese excitability, it is easy to imagine the frantic condition of the little town after Tartarin's abrupt disappearance. ***Et autrement, pas moins, differemment***, they lost their heads, all the more because it was the middle of August and their brains boiled in the sun till their skulls were fit to crack. From morning till night they talked of nothing else; that one name "Tartarin" alone was heard on the pinched lips of the elderly ladies in hoods, in the rosy mouths of grisettes, their hair tied up with velvet ribbons:

"Tartarin, Tartarin..." Even among the plane-trees on the Promenade, heavy with white dust, distracted grasshoppers, vibrating in the sunlight, seemed to strangle with those two sonorous syllables: "Tar.. tar.. tar.. tar.. tar..."

As no one knew anything, naturally every one was well-informed and gave explanations of the departure of the president. Extravagant versions appeared. According to some, he had entered La Trappe; he had eloped with the Dugazon; others declared he had gone to the Isles to found a colony to be called Port-Tarascon, or else to roam Central Africa in search of Livingstone.

"Ah! *vai!* Livingstone!.. Why he has been dead these two years."

But Tarasconese imagination defies all hints of time and space. And the curious thing is that these ideas of La Trappe, colonization, distant travel, were Tartarin's own ideas, dreams of that sleeper awake, communicated in past days to his intimate friends, who now, not knowing what to think, and vexed in their hearts at not being duly informed, affected toward the public the greatest reserve and behaved to one another with a sly air of private understanding. Excourbanies suspected Bravida of being in the secret; Bravida, on his side, thought: "Bezuquet knows the truth; he looks about him like a dog with a bone."

True it was that the apothecary suffered a thousand deaths from this hair-shirt of a secret, which cut him, skinned him, turned him pale and red in the same minute and caused him to squint continually. Remember that he belonged to Tarascon, unfortunate man, and say if, in all martyrology, you can find so terrible a torture as this--the torture of Saint Bezuquet, who knew a secret and could not tell it.

This is why, on that particular evening, in spite of the terrifying news he had just received, his step had something, I hardly know what, freer, more buoyant, as he went to the session of the Club. *Enfin!*.. He was now to speak, to unbosom himself, to tell that which weighed so heavily upon him; and in his haste to unload his breast he cast a few half words as he went along to the loiterers on the Promenade. The day had been so hot, that in spite of the unusual hour (*a quarter to eight* on the clock of the town hall!) and the terrifying darkness, quite a crowd of reckless persons, bourgeois families getting the good of the air while that of their houses evaporated, bands of five or six sewing-women, rambling along in an undulating line of chatter and laughter, were abroad. In every group they were talking of Tartarin.

"*Et autrement*, Monsieur Bezuquet, still no letter?" they asked of the apothecary, stopping him on his way.

"Yes, yes, my friends, yes, there is... Read the *Forum* to-morrow morning..."

He hastened his steps, but they followed him, fastened on him, and along the Promenade rose a murmuring sound, the bleating of a flock, which gathered beneath the windows of the Club, left wide open in great squares of light.

The sessions were held in the *bouillotte* room, where the long table covered with green cloth served as a desk. At the centre, the presidential arm-chair, with P. C. A. embroidered on the back of it; at one end, humbly, the armless chair of the secretary. Behind, the banner of the Club, draped above a long glazed map in relief, on which the Alpines stood up with their respective names and altitudes. Alpenstocks of honour, inlaid with ivory, stacked like billiard cues, ornamented the corners, and a glass-case displayed curiosities, crystals, silex, petrifactions, two porcupines and a salamander, collected on the mountains.

In Tartarin's absence, Costecalde, rejuvenated and radiant, occupied the presidential arm-chair; the armless chair was for Excourbanies, who fulfilled the functions of secretary; but that devil of a man, frizzled, hairy, bearded, was incessantly in need of noise, motion, activity which hindered his sedentary employments. At the smallest pretext, he threw out his arms and legs, uttered fearful howls and "Ha! ha! has!" of ferocious, exuberant joy which always ended with a war-cry in the Tarasconese patois: "***Fen de brut***... let us make a noise "... He was called "the gong" on account of his metallic voice, which cracked the ears of his friends with its ceaseless explosions.

Here and there, on a horsehair divan that ran round the room were the members of the committee.

In the first row, sat the former captain of equipment, Bravida, whom all Tarascon called the Commander; a very small man, clean as a new penny, who redeemed his childish figure by making himself as moustached and savage a head as Vercingetorix.

Next came the long, hollow, sickly face of Pegoulade, the collector, last survivor of the wreck of the "Medusa." Within the memory of man, Tarascon has never been without a last survivor of the wreck of the "Medusa." At one time they even numbered three, who treated one another mutually as impostors, and never con~ sented to meet in the same room. Of these three the only true one was Pegoulade. Setting sail with his parents on the "Medusa," he met with the fatal disaster when six months old,--which did not prevent him from relating the event, *de visu*, in its smallest details, famine, boats, raft, and how he had taken the captain, who was selfishly saving himself, by the throat: "To your duty, wretch!.. "At six months old, ***outre!***... Wearisome, to tell the truth, with that eternal tale which everybody was sick of for the last fifty years; but he took it as a pretext to assume a melancholy air, detached from life: "After what I have seen!" he would say--very unjustly, because it was to that he owed his post as collector and kept it 'under all administrations.

Near him sat the brothers Rognonas, twins and sexagenarians, who never parted, but always quarrelled and said the most monstrous things to each other; their two old heads, defaced, corroded, irregular, and ever looking in opposite directions out of antipathy, were so alike that they might have figured in a collection of coins with IANVS BIFRONS on the exergue.

Here and there, were Judge Bedaride, Barjavel the lawyer, the notary Cambala-lette, and the terrible Doctor Tournatoire, of whom Bravida remarked that he could draw blood from a radish.

In consequence of the great heat, increased by the gas, these gentlemen held the session in their shirt-sleeves, which detracted much from the solemnity of the occasion. It is true that the meeting was a very small one; and the infamous Coste-calde was anxious to profit by that circumstance to fix the earliest possible date for the elections without awaiting Tartarin's return. Confident in this manoeuvre, he was enjoying his triumph in advance, and when, after the reading of the minutes by Excourbanies, he rose to insinuate his scheme, an infernal smile curled up the corners of his thin lips.

"Distrust the man who smiles before he speaks," murmured the Commander.

Costecalde, not flinching, and winking with one eye at the faithful Tourna-toire, began in a spiteful voice:--

"Gentlemen, the extraordinary conduct of our president, the uncertainty in which he leaves us..."

"False!.. The president has written..."

Bezuquet, quivering, planted himself squarely before the table; but conscious that his attitude was anti-parliamentary, he changed his tone, and, raising one hand according to usage, he asked for the floor, to make an urgent communication.

"Speak! Speak!"

Costecalde, very yellow, his throat tightened, gave him the floor by a motion of his head. Then, and not till then, Bezuquet spoke:

"Tartarin is at the foot of the Jungfrau... he is about to make the ascent... he desires to take with him our banner..."

Silence; broken by the heavy breathing of chests; then a loud hurrah, bravos, stamping of the feet, above which rose the gong of Excourbanies uttering his war-cry "Ha! ha! ha! *fen de brut!*" to which the anxious crowd without responded.

Costecalde, getting more and more yellow, tinkled the presidential bell desper-ately. Bezuquet at last was allowed to continue, mopping his forehead and puffing as if he had just mounted five pairs of stairs.

Differemment, the banner that their president requested in order to plant it on virgin heights, should it be wrapped up, packed up, and sent by express like an ordinary trunk?..

"Never!.. Ah! ah! ah!.." roared Excourbanies.

Would it not be better to appoint a delegation--draw lots for three members of the committee?..

He was not allowed to finish. The time to say *zou!* and Bezuquet's proposition was voted by acclamation, and the names of three delegates drawn in the following order: 1, Bravida; 2, Pegoulade; 3, the apothecary.

No. 2, protested. The long journey frightened him, so feeble and ill as he was, *pecherel* ever since that terrible event of the "Medusa."

"I 'll go for you, Pegoulade," roared Excour-banies, telegraphing with all his limbs. As for Bezuquet, he could not leave the pharmacy, the safety of the town depended on him. One imprudence of the pupil, and all Tarascon might be poisoned, decimated:

"*Outre!*" cried the whole committee, agreeing as one man.

Certainly the apothecary could not go himself, but he could send Fascalon; Pascalon could take charge of the banner. That was his business. Thereupon, fresh exclamations, further explosions of the gong, and on the Promenade such a popular tempest that Excourbanies was forced to show himself and address the crowd above its roarings, which his matchless voice soon mastered.

"My friends, Tartarin is found. He is about to cover himself with glory."

Without adding more than "Vive Tartarin!" and his war-cry, given with all the force of his lungs, he stood for a moment enjoying the tremendous clamour of the crowd below, rolling and hustling confusedly in clouds of dust, while from the branches of the trees the grasshoppers added their queer little rattle as if it were broad day.

Hearing all this, Costecalde, who had gone to a window with the rest, returned, staggering, to his arm-chair.

"*Ve!* Costecalde," said some one. "What's the matter with him?.. Look how yellow he is!"

They sprang to him; already the terrible Tournatoire had whipped out his lancet: but the gunsmith, writhing in distress, made a horrible grimace, and said ingenuously:

"Nothing... nothing... let me alone... I know what it is... it is envy."

Poor Costecalde, he seemed to suffer much.

While these things were happening, at the other end of the Tour de Ville, in the pharmacy, Bezuquet's pupil, seated before his master's desk, was patiently patching and gumming together the fragments of Tartarin's letter overlooked by the apothecary at the bottom of the basket. But numerous bits were lacking in the reconstruction, for here is the singular and sinister enigma spread out before him, not unlike a map of Central Africa, with voids and spaces of *terra incognita*, which the artless standard-bearer explored in a state of terrified imagination:

> mad with love reed
> -wick lam
> preserves of Chicago.
> cannot tear myself
> Nihilist
> to death condition
> abom
> in exchange
> for her
> You know me, Ferdi
> know my liberal ideas,
> but from there to tzaricide
> rrible consequences
> Siberia hung
> adore her
> Ah! press thy loyal hand
>
> Tar Tar

VIII.

Memorable dialogue between the jungfrau and Tartarin. A
nihilist salon. The duel with hunting-knives. Frightful
nightmare, "Is it I you are seeking, messieurs?" Strange
reception given by the hotel-keeper Meyer to the Tarasconese
delegation.

Like all the other choice hotels at Interlaken, the Hotel Jungfrau, kept by Meyer, is situated on the Hoeheweg, a wide promenade between double rows of chest-
nut-trees that vaguely reminded Tar-tarin of the beloved Tour de Ville of his native
town, minus the sun, the grasshoppers, and the dust; for during his week's sojourn
at Interlaken the rain had never ceased to fall.

He occupied a very fine chamber with a balcony on the first floor, and trimmed
his beard in the morning before a little hand-glass hanging to the window, an old
habit of his when travelling. The first object that daily struck his eyes beyond the
fields of grass and corn, the nursery gardens, and an amphitheatre of solemn verdure in rising stages, was the Jungfrau, lifting from the clouds her summit, like a
horn, white and pure with unbroken snow, to which was daily clinging a furtive
ray of the still invisible rising sun. Then between the white and rosy Alp and the
Alpinist a little dialogue took place regularly, which was not without its grandeur.

"Tartarin, are you coming?" asked the Jung-frau sternly.

"Here, here..." replied the hero, his thumb under his nose and finishing his
beard as fast as possible. Then he would hastily take down his ascensionist outfit
and, swearing at himself, put it on.

"*Coquin de sort!* there's no name for it..."

But a soft voice rose, demure and clear among the myrtles in the border beneath his window.

"Good-morning," said Sonia, as he appeared upon the balcony, "the landau is
ready... Come, make haste, lazy man..."

"I 'm coming, I 'm coming..."

In a trice he had changed his thick flannel shirt for linen of the finest quality, his mountain knickerbockers for a suit of serpent-green that turned the heads of all the women in Tarascon at the Sunday concerts.

The horses of the landau were pawing before the door; Sonia was already installed beside Boris, paler, more emaciated day by day in spite of the beneficent climate of Interlaken. But, regularly, at the moment of starting, Tartarin was fated to see two forms arise from a bench on the promenade and approach him with the heavy rolling step of mountain bears; these were Rodolphe Kaufmann and Christian Inebnit, two famous Grindelwald guides, engaged by Tartarin for the ascension of the Jungfrau, who came every morning to ascertain if their monsieur were ready to start.

The apparition of these two men, in their iron-clamped shoes and fustian jackets worn threadbare on the back and shoulder by knapsacks and ropes, their naive and serious faces, and the four words of French which they managed to splutter as they twisted their broad-brimmed hats, were a positive torture to Tartarin. In vain he said to them: "Don't trouble yourselves to come; I 'll send for you..."

Every day he found them in the same place and got rid of them by a large coin proportioned to the enormity of his remorse. Enchanted with this method of "doing the Jungfrau," the mountaineers pocketed their **trinkgeld** gravely, and took, with resigned step, the path to their native village, leaving Tartarin confused and despairing at his own weakness. Then the broad open air, the flowering plains reflected in the limpid pupils of Sonia's eyes, the touch of her little foot against his boot in the carriage... The devil take that Jungfrau! The hero thought only of his love, or rather of the mission he had given himself to bring back into the right path that poor little Sonia, so unconsciously criminal, cast by sisterly devotion outside of the law, and outside of human nature.

This was the motive that kept him at Interlaken, in the same hotel as the Wassiliefs. At his age, with his air of a good papa, he certainly could not dream of making that poor child love him, but he saw her so sweet, so brave, so generous to all the unfortunates of her party, so devoted to that brother whom the mines of Siberia had sent back to her, his body eaten with ulcers, poisoned with verdigris, and he himself condemned to death by phthisis more surely than by any court. There was enough in all that to touch a man!

Tartarin proposed to take them to Tarascon and settle them in a villa full of sun at the gates of the town, that good little town where it never rains and where life is spent in fetes and song. And with that he grew excited, rattled a tambourine air on the crown of his hat, and trolled out the gay native chorus of the farandole dance:

Lagadigadeou
La Tarasque, la Tarasque,
Lagadigadeou
La Tarasque de Casteou.

But while a satirical smile pinched still closer the lips of the sick man, Sonia shook her head. Neither fetes nor sun for her so long as the Russians groaned beneath the yoke of the tyrant. As soon as her brother was well--her despairing eyes said another thing--nothing could prevent her from returning up there to suffer and die in the sacred cause.

"But, *coquin de bon sort!*" cried Tartarin, "if you blow up one tyrant there 'll come another... You will have it all to do over again... And the years will go by, *ve!* the days for happiness and love..." His way of saying love--*amour*--a la Tarasconese, with three r's in it and his eyes starting out of his head, amused the young girl; then, serious once more, she declared she would never love any man but the one who delivered her country. Yes, that man, were he as ugly as Bolibine, more rustic and common than Manilof, she was ready to give herself wholly to him, to live at his side, a free gift, as long as her youth lasted and the man wished for her.

"Free gift!" the term used by Nihilists to express those illegal unions they contract among themselves by reciprocal consent. And of such primitive marriage Sonia spoke tranquilly with her virgin air before the Tarasconese, who, worthy bourgeois, peaceful elector, was now ready to spend his days beside that adorable girl in the said state of "free gift" if she had not added those murderous and abominable conditions.

While they were conversing of these extremely delicate matters, the fields, the lakes, the forests, the mountains lay spread before them, and always at each new turn, through the cool mist of that perpetual shower which accompanied our hero on all his excursions, the Jungfrau raised her white crest, as if to poison by remorse those delicious hours. They returned to breakfast at a vast *table d'hote* where the Rices and Prunes continued their silent hostilities, to which Tartarin was wholly indifferent, seated by Sonia, watching that Boris had no open window at his back, assiduous, paternal, exhibiting all his seductions as man of the world and his domestic qualities as an excellent cabbage-rabbit.

After this, he took tea with the Russians in their little salon opening on a tiny garden at the end of the terrace. Another exquisite hour for Tartarin of intimate chat in a low voice while Boris slept on a sofa. The hot water bubbled in the samovar; a perfume of moist flowers slipped through the half-opened door with the blue reflection of the solanums that were clustering about it. A little more sun, more warmth, and here was his dream realized, his pretty Russian installed beside him, taking care of the garden of the baobab.

Suddenly Sonia gave a jump.

"Two o'clock!.. And the letters?"

"I'm going for them," said the good Tartarin, and, merely from the tones of his voice and the resolute, theatrical gesture with which he buttoned his coat and seized his cane, any one would have guessed the gravity of the action, apparently so simple, of going to the post-office to fetch the Wassilief letters.

Closely watched by the local authorities and the Russian police, all Nihilists, but especially their leaders, are compelled to take certain precautions, such as having their letters and papers addressed *poste restante* to simple initials.

Since their installation at Interlaken, Boris being scarcely able to drag himself about, Tartarin, to spare Sonia the annoyance of waiting in line before the post-office wicket exposed to inquisitive eyes, had taken upon himself the risks and perils of this daily nuisance. The post-office is not more than ten minutes' walk from the hotel, in a wide and noisy street at the end of a promenade lined with cafes, breweries, shops for the tourists displaying alpenstocks, gaiters, straps, opera-glasses, smoked glasses, flasks, travelling-bags, all of which articles seemed placed there expressly to shame the renegade Alpinist. Tourists were defiling in caravans, with horses, guides, mules, veils green and blue, and a tintinnabulation of canteens as the animals ambled, the ice-picks marking each step on the cobble-stones. But this festive scene, hourly renewed, left Tartarin indifferent. He never even felt the fresh north wind with a touch of snow coming in gusts from the mountains, so intent was he on baffling the spies whom he supposed to be upon his traces.

The foremost soldier of a vanguard, the sharpshooter skirting the walls of an enemy's town, never advanced with more mistrust than the Taras-conese hero while crossing the short distance between the hotel and the post-office. At the slightest heel-tap sounding behind his own, he stopped, looked attentively at the photographs in the windows, or fingered an English or German book lying on a stall, to oblige the police spy to pass him. Or else he turned suddenly round, to stare with ferocious eyes at a stout servant-girl going to market, or some harmless tourist, a **table d'hote** Prune, who, taking him for a madman, turned off, alarmed, from the sidewalk to avoid him.

When he reached the office, where the wickets open, rather oddly, into the street itself, Tartarin passed and repassed, to observe the surrounding physiognomies before he himself approached: then, suddenly darting forward, he inserted his whole head and shoulders into the opening, muttered a few indistinct syllables (which they always made him repeat, to his great despair), and, possessor at last of the mysterious trust, he returned to the hotel by a great detour on the kitchen side, his hand in his pocket clutching the package of letters and papers, prepared to tear up and swallow everything at the first alarm.

Manilof and Bolibine were usually awaiting his return with the Wassiliefs. They did not lodge in the hotel, out of prudence and economy. Bolibine had found work in a printing-office, and Manilof, a very clever cabinetmaker, was employed by a builder. Tartarin did not like them: one annoyed him by his grimaces and his jeering airs; the other kept looking at him savagely. Besides, they took too much space in Sonia's heart.

"He is a hero!" she said of Bolibine; and she told how for three years he had printed all alone, in the very heart of St. Petersburg, a revolutionary paper. Three years without ever leaving his upper room, or showing himself at a window, sleeping at night in a great cupboard built in the wall, where the woman who lodged him locked him up till morning with his clandestine press.

And then, that life of Manilof, spent for six months in the subterranean passages beneath the Winter Palace, watching his opportunity, sleeping at night on his provision of dynamite, which resulted in giving him frightful headaches, and nervous troubles; all this, aggravated by perpetual anxiety, sudden irruptions of the police, vaguely informed that something was plotting, and coming, suddenly and unexpectedly, to surprise the workmen employed at the Palace. On one of the rare occasions when Manilof came out of the mine, he met on the Place de l'Amiraute a delegate of the Revolutionary Committee, who asked him in a low voice, as he walked along:

"Is it finished?"

"No, not yet..." said the other, scarcely moving his lips. At last, on an evening in February, to the same question in the same words he answered, with the greatest calmness:

"It is finished..."

And almost immediately a horrible uproar confirmed his words, all the lights of the palace went out suddenly, the place was plunged into complete obscurity, rent by cries of agony and terror, the blowing of bugles, the galloping of soldiers, and firemen tearing along with their trucks.

Here Sonia interrupted her tale:

"Is it not horrible, so many human lives sacrificed, such efforts, such courage, such wasted intelligence?.. No, no, it is a bad means, these butcheries in the mass... He who should be killed always escapes... The true way, the most humane, would be to seek the czar himself as you seek the lion, fully determined, fully armed, post yourself at a window or the door of a carriage... and, when he passes....."

"*Be!* yes, *certainemain*..." responded Tartarin embarrassed, and pretending not to seize her meaning; then, suddenly, he would launch into a philosophical, humanitarian discussion with one of the numerous assistants. For Bolibine and Manilof were not the only visitors to the Wassiliefs. Every day new faces appeared of young people, men or women, with the cut of poor students; elated teachers, blond and rosy, with the self-willed forehead and the childlike ferocity of Sonia; outlawed exiles, some of them already condemned to death, which lessened in no way their youthful expansiveness.

They laughed, they talked openly, and as most of them spoke French, Tartarin was soon at his ease. They called him "uncle," conscious of something childlike and artless about him that they liked. Perhaps he was over-ready with his hunting tales; turning up his sleeve to his biceps in order to show the scar of a blow from a panther's claws, or making his hearers feel beneath his beard the holes left there by the fangs of a lion; perhaps also he became too rapidly familiar with these persons, catching them round the waist, leaning on their shoulders, calling them by their Christian names after five minutes' intercourse:

"Listen, Dmitri..." "You know me, Fedor Ivanovich..." They knew him only since yesterday, in any case; but they liked him all the same for his jovial frankness, his amiable, trustful air, and his readiness to please. They read their letters before him, planned their plots, and told their passwords to foil the police: a whole atmosphere of conspiracy which amused the imagination of the Tarasconese hero immensely: so that, however opposed by nature to acts of violence, he could not help, at times, discussing their homicidal plans, approving, criticising, and giving advice dictated by the experience of a great leader who has trod the path of war, trained to the handling of all weapons, and to hand-to-hand conflicts with wild beasts.

One day, when they told in his presence of the murder of a policeman, stabbed by a Nihilist at the theatre, Tartarin showed them how badly the blow had been struck, and gave them a lesson in knifing.

"Like this, *ve!* from the top down. Then there's no risk of wounding yourself..."

And, excited by his own imitation:

"Let's suppose, *te!* that I hold your despot between four eyes in a boar-hunt He is over there, where you are, Fedor, and I'm here, near this round table, each of us with our hunting-knife... Come on, monseigneur, we 'll have it out now..."

Planting himself in the middle of the salon, gathering his sturdy legs under him for a spring, and snorting like a woodchopper, he mimicked a real fight, ending by his cry of triumph as he plunged the weapon to the hilt, from the top down, *coquin de sort!* into the bowels of his adversary.

"That's how it ought to be done, my little fellows!"

But what subsequent remorse! what anguish when, escaping from the magnetism of Sonia's blue eyes, he found himself alone, in his nightcap, alone with his reflections and his nightly glass of *eau sucree!*

Differemment, what was he meddling with? The czar was not his czar, decidedly, and all these matters didn't concern him in the least... And don't you see that some of these days he would be captured, extradited and delivered over to Muscovite justice... **Boufre!** they don't joke, those Cossacks... And in the obscurity of his hotel chamber, with that horrible imaginative faculty which the horizontal position increases, there developed before him--like one of those unfolding pictures given to him in childhood--the various and terrible punishments to which he should be subjected: Tartarin in the verdigris mines, like Boris, working in water to his belly, his body ulcerated, poisoned. He escapes, he hides amid forests laden with snow, pursued by Tartars and bloodhounds trained to hunt men. Exhausted with cold and hunger, he is retaken and finally hung between two thieves, embraced by a pope with greasy hair smelling of brandy and seal-oil; while away down there, at Tarascon in the sunshine, the band playing of a fine Sunday, the crowd, the ungrateful crowd, are installing a radiant Costecalde in the chair of the P. C. A.

It was during the agony of one of these dreadful dreams that he uttered his cry of distress, "Help, help, Bezuquet!" and sent to the apothecary that confidential letter, all moist with the sweat of his nightmare. But Sonia's pretty "Good morning" beneath his window sufficed to cast him back into the weaknesses of indecision.

One evening, returning from the Kursaal to the hotel with the Wassiliefs and Bolibine, after two hours of intoxicating music, the unfortunate man forgot all prudence, and the "Sonia, I love you," which he had so long restrained, was uttered as he pressed the arm that rested on his own. She was not agitated. Perfectly pale, she gazed at him under the gas of the portico on which they had paused: "Then deserve me..." she said, with a pretty enigmatical smile, a smile that gleamed upon her delicate white teeth. Tartarin was about to reply, to bind himself by an oath to some criminal madness when the porter of the hotel came up to him:

"There are persons waiting for you, upstairs... some gentlemen... They want you."

"Want me!.. **Outre!**.. What for?" And No. 1 of his folding series appeared before him: Tartarin captured, extradited... Of course he was frightened, but his attitude was heroic. Quickly detaching himself from Sonia: "Fly, save yourself!" he said to her in a smothered voice. Then he mounted the stairs as if to the scaffold, his head high, his eyes proud, but so disturbed in mind that he was forced to cling to the baluster.

As he entered the corridor, he saw persons grouped at the farther end of it before his door, looking through the keyhole, rapping, and calling out: "Hey! Tartarin..."

He made two steps forward, and said, with parched lips: "Is it I whom you are seeking, messieurs?"

"*Te! pardi*, yes, my president!."

And a little old man, alert and wiry, dressed in gray, and apparently bringing on his coat, his hat, his gaiters and his long and pendent moustache all the dust of his native town, fell upon the neck of the hero and rubbed against his smooth fat cheeks the withered leathery skin of the retired captain of equipment.

"Bravida!.. not possible!.. Excourbanies too!.. and who is that over there?.."

A bleating answered: "Dear ma-a-aster!.." and the pupil advanced, banging against the wall a sort of long fishing-rod with a packet at one end wrapped in gray paper, and oilcloth tied round it with string.

"Hey! *ve!* why it's Pascalon... Embrace me, little one... What's that you are carrying?.. Put it down..."

"The paper... take off the paper!.." whispered Bravida. The youth undid the roll with a rapid hand and the Tarasconese banner was displayed to the eyes of the amazed Tartarin.

The delegates took off their hats.

"President"--the voice of Bravida trembled solemnly--"you asked for the banner and we have brought it, *te!*"

The president opened a pair of eyes as round as apples: "I! I asked for it?"

"What! you did not ask for it? Bezuquet said so.

"Yes, yes, *certainemain*..." said Tartarin, suddenly enlightened by the mention of Bezuquet. He understood all and guessed the rest, and, tenderly moved by the ingenious lie of the apothecary to recall him to a sense of duty and honour, he choked, and stammered in his short beard: "Ah! my children, how kind you are! What good you have done me!"

"*Vive le presidain!*" yelped Pascalon, brandishing the oriflamme. Excourbanies' gong responded, rolling its war-cry (" Ha! ha! ha! *fen de brut*..") to the very cellars of the hotel. Doors opened, inquisitive heads protruded on every floor and then disappeared, alarmed, before that standard and the dark and hairy men who were roaring singular words and tossing their arms in the air. Never had the peaceable Hotel Jungfrau been subjected to such a racket.

"Come into my room," said Tartarin, rather disconcerted. He was feeling about in the darkness to find matches when an authoritative rap on the door made it open of itself to admit the consequential, yellow, and puffy face of the innkeeper Meyer. He was about to enter, but stopped short before the darkness of the room, and said with closed teeth:

"Try to keep quiet... or I 'll have you taken up by the police..."

A grunt as of wild bulls issued from the shadow at that brutal term "taken up." The hotel-keeper recoiled one step, but added: "It is known who you are; they have their eye upon you; for my part, I don't want any more such persons in my house!.."

"Monsieur Meyer," said Tartarin, gently, politely, but very firmly... "Send me my bill... These gentlemen and myself start to-morrow morning for the Jungfrau."

O native soil! O little country within a great one! by only hearing the Tarasconese accent, quivering still with the air of that beloved land beneath the azure folds of its banner, behold Tartarin, delivered from love and its snares and restored to his friends, his mission, his glory.

And now, *zou!*

IX.

At the "Faithful Chamois."

The next day it was charming, that trip on foot from Interlaken to Grindelwald, where they were, in passing, to take guides for the Little Scheideck; charming, that triumphal march of the P. C. A., restored to his trappings and mountain habiliments, leaning on one side on the lean little shoulder of Commander Bravida, and on the other, the robust arm of Excourbanies, proud, both of them, to be nearest to him, to support their dear president, to carry his ice-axe, his knapsack, his alpenstock, while sometimes before, sometimes behind or on their flanks the fanatical Pascalon gambolled like a puppy, his banner duly rolled up into a package to avoid the tumultuous scenes of the night before.

The gayety of his companions, the sense of duty accomplished, the Jungfrau all white upon the sky, over there, like a vapour--nothing short of all this could have made the hero forget what he left behind him, for ever and ever it may be, and without farewell. However, at the last houses of Interlaken his eyelids swelled and, still walking on, he poured out his feelings in turn into the bosom of Excourbanies: "Listen, Spiridion," or that of Bravida: "You know me, Placide..." For, by an irony on nature, that indomitable warrior was called Placide, and that rough buffalo, with all his instincts material, Spiridion.

Unhappily, the Tarasconese race, more gallant than sentimental, never takes its love-affairs very seriously. "Whoso loses a woman and ten sous, is to be pitied about the money..." replied the sententious Placide to Tartarin's tale, and Spiridion thought exactly like him. As for the innocent Pascalon, he was horribly afraid of women, and reddened to the ears when the name of the Little Scheideck was uttered before him, thinking some lady of flimsy morals was referred to. The poor lover was therefore reduced to keep his confidences to himself, and console himself alone--which, after all, is the surest way.

But what grief could have resisted the attractions of the way through that narrow, deep and sombre valley, where they walked on the banks of a winding river all white with foam, rumbling with an echo like thunder among the pine-woods which skirted both its shores.

The Tarasconese delegation, their heads in the air, advanced with a sort of religious awe and admiration, like the comrades of Sinbad the Sailor when they stood before the mangoes, the cotton-trees, and all the giant flora of the Indian coasts. Knowing nothing but their own little bald and stony mountains they had never imagined there could be so many trees together or such tall ones.

"That is nothing, as yet... wait till you see the Jungfrau," said the P. C. A., who enjoyed their amazement and felt himself magnified in their eyes.

At the same time, as if to brighten the scene and humanize its solemn note, cavalcades went by them, great landaus going at full speed, with veils floating from the doorways where curious heads leaned out to look at the delegation pressing round its president. From point to point along the roadside were booths spread with knick-knacks of carved wood, while young girls, stiff in their laced bodices, their striped skirts and broad-brimmed straw hats, were offering bunches of strawberries

and edelweiss. Occasionally, an Alpine horn sent among the mountains its melancholy ritornello, swelling, echoing from gorge to gorge, and slowly diminishing,
like a cloud that dissolves into vapour.

"'T is fine, 't is like an organ," murmured Pascalon, his eyes moist, in ecstasy,
like the stained-glass saint of a church window. Excourbanies roared, undiscour-
aged, and the echoes repeated, till sight and sound were lost, his Tarasconese intonations: "Ha! ha! ha! *fen de brut!*"

But people grow weary after marching for two hours through the same sort of
decorative scene, however well it may be organized, green on blue, glaciers in the
distance, and all things sonorous as a musical clock. The dash of the torrents, the
singers in triplets, the sellers of carved objects, the little flower-girls, soon became
intolerable to our friends,--above all, the dampness, the steam rising in this species
of tunnel, the soaked soil full of water-plants, where never had the sun penetrat-
ed.

"It is enough to give one a pleurisy," said Bravida, turning up the collar of his
coat. Then weariness set in, hunger, ill-humour. They could find no inn; and presently Excourbanies and Bravida, having stuffed themselves with strawberries, began
to suffer cruelly. Pascalon himself, that angel, bearing not only the banner, but the
ice-axe, the knapsack, the alpenstock, of which the others had rid themselves basely
upon him, even Pascalon had lost his gayety and ceased his lively gambolling.

At a turn of the road, after they had just crossed the Lutschine by one of those
covered bridges that are found in regions of deep snow, a loud blast on a horn
greeted them.

"Ah! *vai*, enough!.. enough!" howled the exasperated delegation.

The man, a giant, ensconced by the roadside, let go an enormous trumpet of
pine wood reaching to the ground and ending there in a percussion-box, which
gave to this prehistoric instrument the sonorousness of a piece of artillery.

"Ask him if he knows of an inn," said the president to Excourbanies, who, with
enormous cheek and a small pocket dictionary undertook, now that they were in
German Switzerland, to serve the delegation as interpreter. But before he could pull
out his dictionary the man replied in very good French:

"An inn, messieurs? Why certainly... The 'Faithful Chamois' is close by; allow
me to show you the place."

On the way, he told them he had lived in Paris for several years, as commissionnaire at the corner of the rue Vivienne.

"Another employe of the Company, *parbleu!*" thought Tartarin, leaving his friends to be surprised. However, Bompard's comrade was very useful, for, in spite of its French sign, *Le Chamois Fidele* the people of the "Faithful Chamois" could speak nothing but a horrible German patois.

Presently, the Tarasconese delegation, seated around an enormous potato omelet, recovered both the health and the good-humour as essential to Southerners as the sun of their skies. They drank deep, they ate solidly. After many toasts to the president and his coming ascension, Tartarin, who had puzzled over the tavern-sign ever since his arrival, inquired of the horn-player, who was breaking a crust in a corner of the room:

"So you have chamois here, it seems?.. I thought there were none left in Switzerland."

The man winked:

"There are not many, but enough to let you see them now and then."

"Shoot them, is what he wants, *ve*" said Pas-calon, full of enthusiasm; "never did the president miss a shot!"

Tartarin regretted that he had not brought his carbine.

"Wait a minute, and I 'll speak to the landlord."

It so happened that the landlord was an old chamois hunter; he offered his gun, his powder, his buck-shot, and even himself as guide to a haunt he knew.

"Forward, *zou!*" cried Tartarin, granting to his happy Alpinists the opportunity to show off the prowess of their chief. It was only a slight delay, after all; the Jungfrau lost nothing by waiting.

Leaving the inn at the back, they had only to walk through an orchard, no bigger than the garden of a station-master, before they found themselves on a mountain, gashed with great crevasses, among the fir-trees and underbrush.

The innkeeper took the advance, and the Taras-conese presently saw him far up the height, waving his arms and throwing stones, no doubt to rouse the chamois. They rejoined him with much pain and difficulty over that rocky slope, hard especially to persons who had just been eating and were as little used to climbing as these good Alpinists of Tarascon. The air was heavy, moreover, with a tempest breath that was slowly rolling the clouds along the summits above their heads.

"**Boufre!**" groaned Bravida.

Excourbanies growled: "**Outre!**"

"What shall I be made to say!" added the gentle, bleating Pascalon.

But the guide having, by a violent gesture, ordered them to hold their tongues, and not to stir, Tartarin remarked, "Never speak under arms," with a sternness that rebuked every one, although the president alone had a weapon. They stood stock still, holding their breaths. Suddenly, Pas-calon cried out:

"**Ve** the chamois, **ve**.."

About three hundred feet above them, the upright horns, the light buff coat and the four feet gathered together of the pretty creature stood defined like a carved image at the edge of the rock, looking at them fearlessly. Tartarin brought his piece to his shoulder methodically, as his habit was, and was just about to fire when the chamois disappeared.

"It is your fault," said the Commander to Pascalon... "you whistled... and that frightened him."

"I whistled!.. I?"

"Then it was Spiridion..."

"Ah, **vai!** never in my life."

Nevertheless, they had all heard a whistle, strident, prolonged. The president settled the question by relating how the chamois, at the approach of enemies, gives a sharp danger signal through the nostrils. That devil of a Tartarin knew everything about this kind of hunt, as about all others!

At the call of their guide they started again; but the acclivity became steeper and steeper, the rocks more ragged, with bogs between them to right and left. Tartarin kept the lead, turning constantly to help the delegates, holding out his hand or his carbine: "Your hand, your hand, if you don't mind," cried honest Bravida, who was very much afraid of loaded weapons.

Another sign of the guide, another stop of the delegation, their noses in the air.

"I felt a drop!" murmured the Commander, very uneasy. At the same instant the thunder growled, but louder than the thunder roared the voice of Excourbanies: "Fire, Tartarin!" and the chamois bounded past them, crossing the ravine like a golden flash, too quickly for Tartarin to take aim, but not so fast that they did not hear that whistle of his nostrils.

"I 'll have him yet, **coquin de sort!**" cried the president, but the delegates protested. Excourbanies, becoming suddenly very sour, demanded if he had sworn to exterminate them.

"Dear ma-a-aster," bleated Pascalon, timidly, "I have heard say that chamois if you corner them in abysses turn at bay against the hunter and are very dangerous."

"Then don't let us corner him!" said Bravida hastily.

Tartarin called them milksops. But while they were arguing, suddenly, abruptly, they all disappeared from one another's gaze in a warm thick vapour that smelt of sulphur, through which they sought each other, calling:

"Hey! Tartarin."

"Are you there, Placide?"

"Ma-a-as-ter!"

"Keep cool! Keep cool!"

A regular panic. Then a gust of wind broke through the mist and whirled it away like a torn veil clinging to the briers, through which a zigzag flash of lightning fell at their feet with a frightful clap of thunder. "My cap!" cried Spiridion, as the tempest bared his head, its hairs erect and crackling with electric sparks. They were in the very heart of the storm, the forge itself of Vulcan. Bravida was the first to fly, at full speed, the rest of the delegation flew behind him, when a cry from the president, who thought of everything, stopped them:

"Thunder!.. beware of the thunder!.."

At any rate, outside of the very real danger of which he warned them, there was no possibility of running on those steep and gullied slopes, now transformed into torrents, into cascades, by the pouring rain. The return was awful, by slow steps under that crazy cliff, amid the sharp, short flashes of lightning followed by explosions, slipping, falling, and forced at times to halt. Pascalon crossed himself and invoked aloud, as at Tarascon: "Sainte Marthe and Sainte Helene, Sainte Marie-Madeleine," while Excourbanies swore: "**Coquin de sort!**" and Bravida, the rearguard, looked back in trepidation:

"What the devil is that behind us?.. It is galloping... it is whistling... there, it has stopped..."

The idea of a furious chamois flinging itself upon its hunters was in the mind of the old warrior. In a low voice, in order not to alarm the others, he communicated his fears to Tartarin, who bravely took his place as the rearguard and marched along, soaked to the skin, his head high, with that mute determination which is given by the imminence of danger. But when he reached the inn and saw his dear Alpinists under shelter, drying their wet things, which smoked around a huge porcelain stove in a first floor chamber, to which rose an odour of grog already ordered, the president shivered and said, looking very pale: "I believe I have taken cold."

"Taken cold!" No question now of starting again; the delegation asked only for rest Quick, a bed was warmed, they hurried the hot wine grog, and after his second glass the president felt throughout his comfort-loving body a warmth, a tingling that augured well. Two pillows at his back, a "*plumeau*" on his feet, his muffler round his head, he experienced a delightful sense of well-being in listening to the roaring of the storm, inhaling that good pine odour of the rustic little room with its wooden walls and leaden panes, and in looking at his dear Alpinists, gathered, glass in hand, around his bed in the anomalous character given to their Gallic, Roman or Saracenic types by the counterpanes, curtains, and carpets in which they were bundled while their own clothes steamed before the stove. Forgetful of himself, he questioned each of them in a sympathetic voice:

"Are you well, Placide?.. Spiridion, you seemed to be suffering just now?.."

No, Spiridion suffered no longer, all that had passed away on seeing the president so ill. Bravida, who adapted moral truths to the proverbs of his nation, added cynically: "**Neighbour's ill comforts, and even cures.**" Then they talked of their hunt, exciting one another with the recollection of certain dangerous episodes, such as the moment when the animal turned upon them furiously; and without complicity of lying, in fact, most ingenuously, they fabricated the fable they afterwards related on their return to Tarascon.

Suddenly, Pascalon, who had been sent in search of another supply of grog, reappeared in terror, one arm out of the blue-flowered curtain that he gathered about him with the chaste gesture of a Polyeucte. He was more than a second before he could articulate, in a whisper, breathlessly: "The chamois!.."

"Well, what of the chamois?.."

"He's down there, in the kitchen... warming himself..."

"Ah! *vai*..."

"You are joking..."

"Suppose you go and see, Placide."

Bravida hesitated. Excourbanies descended on the tips of his toes, but returned almost immediately, his face convulsed... More and more astounding!.. the chamois was drinking grog.

They certainly owed it to him, poor beast, after the wild run he had been made to take on the mountain, dispatched and recalled by his master, who, as a usual thing, put him through his evolutions in the house, to show to tourists how easily a chamois could be trained.

"It is overwhelming!" said Bravida, making no further effort at comprehension; as for Tartarin, he dragged the muffler over his eyes like a nightcap to hide from the delegates the soft hilarity that overcame him at encountering wherever he went the dodges and the performers of Bompard's Switzerland.

X.

The ascension of the Jungfrau. Ve! the oxen. The Kennedy crampons will not work. Nor the reedlamp either. Apparition of masked men at the chalet of the Alpine Club. The president in a crevasse. On the summit. Tartarin becomes a god.

Great influx, that morning, to the Hotel Bellevue on the Little Scheideck. In spite of the rain and the squalls, tables had been laid outside in the shelter of the veranda, amid a great display of alpenstocks, flasks, telescopes, cuckoo clocks in carved wood, so that tourists could, while breakfasting, contemplate at a depth of six thousand feet before them the wonderful valley of Grindel-wald on the left, that of Lauterbrunnen on the right, and opposite, within gunshot as it seemed, the immaculate, grandiose slopes of the Jungfrau, its *neves*, glaciers, all that reverberating whiteness which illumines the air about it, making glasses more transparent, and linen whiter.

But now, for a time, general attention was attracted to a noisy, bearded cara-van, which had just arrived on horse, mule, and donkey-back, also in a *chaise a porteurs*, who had prepared themselves to climb the mountain by a copious break-fast, and were now in a state of hilarity, the racket of which contrasted with the bored and solemn airs of the very distinguished Rices and Prunes collected on the Scheideck, such as: Lord Chipendale, the Belgian senator and his family, the Aus-tro-Hungarian diplomat, and several others. It would certainly have been supposed that the whole party of these bearded men sitting together at table were about to attempt the ascension, for one and all were busy with preparations for departure, rising, rushing about to give directions to the guides, inspecting the provisions, and calling to each other from end to end of the terrace in stentorian tones.

"Hey! Placide, *ve!* the cooking-pan, see if it is in the knapsack!.. Don't forget the reed-lamp, *au mouain*."

Not until the actual departure took place was it seen that, of all the caravan, only one was to make the ascension: but which one?

"Children, are we ready?" said the good Tar-tarin in a joyous, triumphant voice, in which not a shade of anxiety trembled at the possible dangers of the trip--his last doubt as to the Company's manipulation of Switzerland being dissipated that very morning before the two glaciers of Grindel-wald each protected by a wicket and a turnstile, with this inscription "Entrance to the glacier: one franc fifty."

He could, therefore, enjoy without anxiety this departure in apotheosis, the joy of feeling himself looked at, envied, admired by those bold little misses in boys' caps who laughed at him so prettily on the Rigi-Kulm, and were now enthusiastically comparing his short person with the enormous mountain he was about to climb. One drew his portrait in her album, another sought the honour of touching his al-penstock. "Tchemppegne!.. Tchemppegne!.." called out of a sudden a tall, funereal Englishman with a brick-coloured skin, coming up to him, bottle and glass in hand. Then, after obliging the hero to drink with him:

"Lord Chipendale, sir... And you?"

"Tartarin of Tarascon."

"Oh! yes... Tartarine... Capital name for a horse," said the lord, who must have been one of those great turfmen across the Channel.

The Austro-Hungarian diplomat also came to press the Alpinist's hand between his mittens, remembering vaguely to have seen him somewhere. "Enchanted!.. enchanted!.." he enunciated several times, and then, not knowing how to get out of it, he added: "My compliments to madame..." his social formula for cutting short presentations.

But the guides were impatient; they must reach before nightfall the hut of the Alpine Club, where they were to sleep for the first stage, and there was not a minute to lose. Tartarin felt it, saluted all with a circular gesture, smiled at the malicious misses, and then, in a voice of thunder, commanded:

"Pascalon, the banner!"

It waved to the breeze; the Southerners took off their hats, for they love theatricals at Tarascon; and at the cry, a score of times repeated: "Long live the president!.. Long live Tartarin!.. Ah! ah!..*fen de brut!*.." the column moved off, the two guides in front carrying the knapsack, the provisions, and a supply of wood; then came Pascalon bearing the oriflamme, and lastly the P. C. A. with the delegates who proposed to accompany him as far as the glacier of the Guggi.

Thus deployed in procession, bearing its flapping flag along the sodden way beneath those barren or snowy crests, the cortege vaguely recalled the funeral marches of an All Souls' day in the country.

Suddenly the Commander cried out, alarmed: "*Ve!* those oxen!"

Some cattle were now seen browsing the short grass in the hollows of the ground. The former captain of equipment had a nervous and quite insurmountable terror of those animals, and as he could not be left alone the delegation was forced to stop. Pascalon transmitted the standard to the guides. Then, with a last embrace, hasty injunctions, and one eye on the cows:

"Adieu, adieu, *que!*"

"No imprudence, *au mouain*..." they parted. As for proposing to the president to go up with him, no one even thought of it; 'twas so high, *boufre!* And the nearer they came to it the higher it grew, the abysses were more abysmal, the peaks bristled up in a white chaos, which looked to be insurmountable. It was better to look at the ascension from the Scheideck.

In all his life, naturally, the president of the Club of the Alpines had never set foot on a glacier. There is nothing of that sort on the mountainettes of Tarascon, little hills as balmy and dry as a packet of lavender; and yet the approaches to the Guggi gave him the impression of having already seen them, and wakened recollections of hunts in Provence at the end of the Camargue, near to the sea. The same turf always getting shorter and parched, as if seared by fire. Here and there were puddles of water, infiltrations of the ground betrayed by puny reeds, then came the moraine, like a sandy dune full of broken shells and cinders, and, far at the end, the glacier, with its blue-green waves crested with white and rounded in form, a silent, congealed ground-swell. The wind which came athwart it, whistling and strong, had the same biting, salubrious freshness as his own sea-breeze.

"No, thank you... I have my crampons..." said Tartarin to the guide, who offered him woollen socks to draw on over his boots; "Kennedy crampons... perfected... very convenient..." He shouted, as if to a deaf person, in order to make himself understood by Christian Inebnit, who knew no more French than his comrade Kaufmann; and then the P. C. A. sat down upon the moraine and strapped on a species of sandal with three enormous and very strong iron spikes. He had practised them a hundred times, these Kennedy crampons, manoeuvring them in the garden of the baobab; nevertheless, the present effect was unexpected. Beneath the weight of the hero the spikes were driven into the ice with such force that all efforts to withdraw them were vain. Behold him, therefore, nailed to the glacier, sweating, swearing, making with arms and alpenstock most desperate gymnastics and reduced finally to shouting for his guides, who had gone forward, convinced that they had to do with an experienced Alpinist.

Under the impossibility of uprooting him, they undid the straps, and, the crampons, abandoned in the ice, being replaced by a pair of knitted socks, the president continued his way, not without much difficulty and fatigue. Unskilful in holding his stick, his legs stumbled over it, then its iron point skated and dragged him along if he leaned upon it too heavily. He tried the ice-axe--still harder to manoeuvre, the swell of the glacier increasing by degrees, and pressing up, one above another, its motionless waves with all the appearance of a furious and petrified tempest.

Apparent immobility only, for hollow crackings, subterranean gurgles, enormous masses of ice displacing themselves slowly, as if moved by the machinery of a stage, indicated the inward life of this frozen mass and its treacherous elements. To the eyes of our Alpinist, wherever he cast his axe crevasses were opening, bottomless pits, where masses of ice in fragments rolled indefinitely. The hero fell repeatedly; once to his middle in one of those greenish gullies, where his broad shoulders alone kept him from going to the bottom.

On seeing him so clumsy, and yet so tranquil, so sure of himself, laughing, singing, gesticulating, as he did while breakfasting, the guides imagined that Swiss champagne had made an impression upon him. What else could they suppose of the president of an Alpine Club, a renowned ascensionist, of whom his friends spoke only with "Ahs!" and exultant gestures. After taking him each by the arm with the respectful firmness of policemen putting into a carriage an overcome heir to a title, they endeavoured, by the help of monosyllables and gestures, to rouse his mind to a sense of the dangers of the route, the necessity of reaching the hut before nightfall, with threats of crevasses, cold, avalanches. Finally, with the point of their ice-picks they showed him the enormous accumulation of ice, of *neve* not yet transformed into glacier rising before them to the zenith in blinding repetition.

But the worthy Tartarin laughed at all that: "Ha! *vai!* crevasses!.. Ha! *vai!* those avalanches!.." and he burst out laughing, winked his eye, and prodded their sides with his elbows to let them know they could not fool him, for *he* was in the secret of the comedy.

The guides at last ended by making merry with the Tarasconese songs, and when they rested a moment on a solid block to let their monsieur get his breath, they yodelled in the Swiss way, though not too loudly, for fear of avalanches, nor very long, for time was getting on. They knew the coming of night by the sharper cold, but especially by the singular change in hue of these snows and ice-packs, heaped-up, overhanging, which always keep, even under misty skies, a rainbow tinge of colour until the daylight fades, rising higher and higher to the vanishing summits, where the snows take on the livid, spectral tints of the lunar universe. Pallor, petrifaction, silence, death itself. And the good Tartarin, so warm, so living, was beginning to lose his liveliness when the distant cry of a bird, the note of a "snow partridge" brought back before his eyes a baked landscape, a copper-coloured setting sun, and a band of Taras-conese sportsmen, mopping their faces, seated on their empty game-bags, in the slender shade of an olive-tree. The recollection was a comfort to him.

At the same moment Kaufmann pointed to something that looked like a faggot of wood on the snow. 'T was the hut. It seemed as if they could get to it in a few strides, but, in point of fact, it took a good half-hour's walking. One of the guides went on ahead to light the fire. Darkness had now come on; the north wind rattled on the cadaverous way, and Tartarin, no longer paying attention to anything, supported by the stout arm of the mountaineer, stumbled and bounded along without a dry thread on him in spite of the falling temperature. All of a sudden a flame shot up before him, together with an appetizing smell of onion soup.

They were there.

Nothing can be more rudimentary than these halting-places established on the mountains by the Alpine Club of Switzerland. A single room, in which an inclined plane of hard wood serves as a bed and takes up nearly all the space, leaving but little for the stove and the long table, screwed to the floor like the benches that are round it. The table was already laid; three bowls, pewter spoons, the reed-lamp to heat the coffee, two cans of Chicago preserved meats already opened. Tartarin thought the dinner delicious although the fumes of the onion soup infected the atmosphere, and the famous spirit-lamp, which ought to have made its pint of coffee in three minutes, refused to perform its functions.

At the dessert he sang; that was his only means of conversing with his guides. He sang them the airs of his native land: **La Tarasque**, and **Les Filles d'Avignon**. To which the guides responded with local songs in German patois: **Mi Vater isch en Appenzeller... aou... aou**... Worthy fellows with hard, weather-beaten features as if cut from the rock, beards in the hollows that looked like moss and those clear eyes, used to great spaces, like the eyes of sailors. The same sensation of the sea and the open, which he had felt just now on approaching Guggi, Tartarin again felt here, in presence of these mariners of the glacier in this close cabin, low and smoky, the regular forecastle of a ship; in the dripping of the snow from the roof as it melted with the warmth; in the great gusts of wind, shaking everything, cracking the boards, fluttering the flame of the lamp, and falling abruptly into vast, unnatural silence, like the end of the world.

They had just finished dinner when heavy steps upon the ringing path and voices were heard approaching. Violent blows with the butt end of some weapon shook the door. Tartarin, greatly excited, looked at his guides... A nocturnal attack on these heights!.. The blows redoubled. "Who goes there?" cried the hero, jumping for his ice-axe; but already the hut was invaded by two gigantic Yankees, in white linen masks, their clothing soaked with snow and sweat, and behind them guides, porters, a whole caravan, on its return from ascending the Jungfrau.

"You are welcome, milords," said Tartarin, with a liberal, dispensing gesture, of which the milords showed not the slightest need in making themselves free of everything. In a trice the table was surrounded, the dishes removed, the bowls and spoons rinsed in hot water for the use of the new arrivals (according to established custom in Alpine huts); the boots of the milords smoked before the stove, while they themselves, bare-footed, their feet wrapped in straw, were sprawling at their ease before a fresh onion soup.

Father and son, these two Americans; two red-haired giants, with heads of pioneers, hard and self-reliant. One of them, the elder, had two dilated eyes, almost white, in a bloated, sun-burned, fissured face, and presently, by the hesitating way in which he groped for his bowl and spoon, and the care with which his son looked after him, Tartarin became aware that this was the famous blind Alpinist of whom he had been told, not believing the tale, at the Hotel Bellevue; a celebrated climber in his youth, who now, in spite of his sixty years and his infirmity, was going over with his son the scenes of his former exploits. He had already done the Wetter-horn and the Jungfrau, and was intending to attack the Matterhorn and the Mont Blanc, declaring that the air upon summits, that glacial breath with its taste of snow, caused him inexpressible joy, and a perfect recall of his lost vigour.

"*Differemment*," asked Tartarin of one of the porters, for the Yankees were not communicative, and answered only by a "yes" or a "no" to all his advances "*differ-emment* inasmuch as he can't see, how does he manage at the dangerous places?"

"Oh! he has got the mountaineer's foot; besides, his son watches over him, and places his heels... And it is a fact that he has never had an accident."

"All the more because accidents in Switzerland are never very terrible, *que?*" With a comprehending smile to the puzzled porter, Tartarin, more and more convinced that the "whole thing was *blague*," stretched himself out on the plank rolled in his blanket, the muffler up to his eyes, and went to sleep, in spite of the light, the noise, the smoke of the pipes and the smell of the onion soup...

"Mossie!.. Mossie!.."

One of his guides was shaking him for departure, while the other poured boiling coffee into the bowls. A few oaths and the groans of sleepers whom Tartarin crushed on his way to the table, and then to the door. Abruptly he found himself outside, stung by the cold, dazzled by the fairy-like reflections of the moon upon that white expanse, those motionless congealed cascades, where the shadow of the peaks, the *aiguilles*, the *seracs*, were sharply defined in the densest black. No longer the sparkling chaos of the afternoon, nor the livid rising upward of the gray tints of evening, but a strange irregular city of darksome alleys, mysterious passages, doubtful corners between marble monuments and crumbling ruins--a dead city, with broad desert spaces.

Two o'clock! By walking well they could be at the top by mid-day. "*Zou!*" said the P. C. A., very lively, and dashing forward, as if to the assault. But his guides stopped him. They must be roped for the dangerous passages.

"Ah! *vai*, roped!.. Very good, if that amuses you."

Christian Inebnit took the lead, leaving twelve feet of rope between himself and Tartarin, who was separated by the same length from the second guide who carried the provisions and the banner. The hero kept his footing better than he did the day before; and confidence in the Company must indeed have been strong, for he did not take seriously the difficulties of the path--if we can call a path the terrible ridge of ice along which they now advanced with precaution, a ridge but a few feet wide and so slippery that Christian was forced to cut steps with his ice-axe.

The line of the ridge sparkled between two depths of abysses on either side. But if you think that Tartarin was frightened, not at all! Scarcely did he feel the little quiver of the cuticle of a freemason novice when subjected to his opening test. He placed his feet most precisely in the holes which the first guide cut for them, doing all that he saw the guide do, as tranquil as he was in the garden of the baobab when he practised around the margin of the pond, to the terror of the goldfish. At one place the ridge became so narrow that he was forced to sit astride of it, and while they went slowly forward, helping themselves with their hands, a loud detonation echoed up, on their right, from beneath them. "Avalanche!" said Inebnit, keeping motionless till the repercussion of the echoes, numerous, grandiose, filling the sky, died away at last in a long roll of thunder in the far distance, where the final detonation was lost. After which, silence once more covered all as with a winding-sheet.

The ridge passed, they went up a *neve* the slope of which was rather gentle but its length interminable. They had been climbing nearly an hour when a slender pink line began to define the summits far, far above their heads. It was the dawn, thus announcing itself. Like a true Southerner, enemy to shade, Tartarin trolled out his liveliest song:

Grand souleu de la Provenco
Gai compaire dou mistrau--
A violent shake of the rope from before and behind stopped him short in the middle of his couplet. "Hush... Hush..." said Inebnit, pointing with his ice-axe to the threatening line of gigantic *seracs* on their tottering foundations which the slightest jar might send thundering down the steep. But Tartarin knew what *that* meant; he was not the man to ply with any such tales, and he went on singing in a resounding voice:

Tu qu 'escoules la Duranco
Commo un flot de vin de Crau.
The guides, seeing that they could not silence their crazy singer, made a great detour to get away from the *seracs*, and presently were stopped by an enormous crevasse, the glaucous green sides of which were lighted, far down their depths, by the first furtive rays of the dawn. What is called in Switzerland "a snow bridge" spanned it; but so slight was it, so fragile, that they had scarcely advanced a step before it crumbled away in a cloud of white dust, dragging down the leading guide and Tartarin, hanging to the rope which Rodolphe Kaufmann, the rear guide, was alone left to hold, clinging with all the strength of his mountain vigour to his pick-axe, driven deeply into the ice. But although he was able to hold the two men suspended in the gulf he had not enough force to draw them up and he remained, crouching on the snow, his teeth clenched, his muscles straining, and too far from the crevasse to see what was happening.

Stunned at first by the fall, and blinded by snow, Tartarin waved his arms and legs at random, like a puppet out of order; then, drawing himself up by means of the rope, he hung suspended over the abyss, his nose against its icy side, which his breath polished, in the attitude of a plumber in the act of soldering a waste-pipe.

He saw the sky above him growing paler and the stars disappearing; below he could fathom the gulf and its opaque shadows, from which rose a chilling breath.

Nevertheless, his first bewilderment over, he recovered his self-possession and his fine good-humour.

"Hey! up there! *pere* Kaufmann, don't leave us to mildew here, *que!* there 's a draught all round, and besides, this cursed rope is cutting our loins."

Kaufmann was unable to answer; to have unclenched his teeth would have lessened his strength. But Inebnit shouted from below:

"Mossie... Mossie... ice-axe..." for his own had been lost in the fall; and, the heavy implement being now passed from the hands of Tartarin to those of the guide (with difficulty, owing to the space that separated the two hanged ones), the mountaineer used it to make notches in the ice-wall before him, into which he could fasten both hands and feet.

The weight of the rope being thus lessened by at least one-half, Rodolphe Kaufmann, with carefully calculated vigour and infinite precautions, began to draw up the president, whose Tarasconese cap appeared at last at the edge of the crevasse. Inebnit followed him in turn and the two mountaineers met again with that effusion of brief words which, in persons of limited elocution, follows great dangers. Both were trembling with their effort, and Tartarin passed them his flask of kirsch to steady their legs. He himself was nimble and calm, and while he shook himself free of snow he hummed his song under the nose of his wondering guides, beating time with his foot to the measure:

"*Brav... brav... Franzose...*" said Kaufmann, tapping him on the shoulder; to which Tartarin answered with his fine laugh:

"You rogue! I knew very well there was no danger..."

Never within the memory of guides was there seen such an Alpinist.

They started again, climbing perpendicularly a sort of gigantic wall of ice some thousand feet high, in which they were forced to cut steps as they went along, which took much time. The man of Tarascon began to feel his strength give way under the brilliant sun which flooded the whiteness of the landscape and was all the more fatiguing to his eyes because he had dropped his green spectacles into the crevasse. Presently, a dreadful sense of weakness seized him, that mountain sickness which produces the same effects as sea-sickness. Exhausted, his head empty, his legs flaccid, he stumbled and lost his feet, so that the guides were forced to grasp him, one on each side, supporting and hoisting him to the top of that wall of ice. Scarcely three hundred feet now separated them from the summit of the Jungfrau; but although the snow was hard and bore them, and the path much easier, this last stage took an almost interminable time, the fatigue and the suffocation of the P. C. A. increasing all the while.

Suddenly the mountaineers loosed their hold upon him, and waving their caps began to yodel in a transport of joy. They were there! This spot in immaculate space, this white crest, somewhat rounded, was the goal, and for that good Tartarin the end of the somnambulic torpor in which he had wandered for an hour or more.

"Scheideck! Scheideck!" shouted the guides, showing him far, far below, on a verdant plateau emerging from the mists of the valley, the Hotel Bellevue about the size of a thimble.

Thence to where they stood lay a wondrous panorama, an ascent of fields of gilded snow, oranged by the sun, or else of a deep, cold blue, a piling up of mounds of ice, fantastically structured into towers, *fleches, aiguilles, aretes*, and gigantic heaps, under which one could well believe that the lost megatherium or mastodon lay sleeping. All the tints of the rainbow played there and met in the bed of vast glaciers rolling down their immovable cascades, crossed by other little frozen torrents, the surfaces of which the sun's warmth liquefied, making them smoother and more glittering. But, at the great height at which they stood, all this sparkling brilliance calmed itself; a light floated, cold, ecliptic, which made Tartarin shudder even more than the sense of silence and solitude in that white desert with its mysterious recesses.

A little smoke, with hollow detonations, rose from the hotel. They were seen, a cannon was fired in their honour, and the thought that they were being looked at, that his Alpinists were there, and the misses, the illustrious Prunes and Rices, all with their opera-glasses levelled up to him, recalled Tartarin to a sense of the grandeur of his mission. He tore thee, O Tarasconese banner! from the hands of the guide, waved thee twice or thrice, and then, plunging the handle of his ice-axe deep into the snow, he seated himself upon the iron of the pick, banner in hand, superb, facing the public. And there--unknown to himself--by one of those spectral reflections frequent upon summits, taken between the sun and the mists that rose behind him, a gigantic Tartarin was outlined on the sky, broader, dumpier, his beard bristling beyond the muffler, like one of those Scandinavian gods enthroned, as the legend has it, among the clouds.

XI.

En route for Tarascon. The Lake of Geneva. Tartarin proposes a visit to the dungeon of Bonnivard. Short dialogue amid the roses. The whole band under lock and key. The unfortunate Bonnivard. Where the rope made at Avignon was found.

As a result of the ascension, Tartarin's nose peeled, pimpled, and his cheeks cracked. He kept to his room in the Hotel Bellevue for five days--five days of salves and compresses, the sticky unsavouriness and ennui of which he endeavoured to elude by playing cards with the delegates or dictating to them a long, circumstantial account of his expedition, to be read in session, before the Club of the Alpines and published in the *Forum*. Then, as the general lumbago had disappeared and nothing remained upon the noble countenance of the P. C. A. but a few blisters, sloughs and chilblains on a fine complexion of Etruscan pottery, the delegation and its president set out for Tarascon, via Geneva.

Let me omit the episodes of that journey, the alarm cast by the Southern band into narrow railway carriages, steamers, *tables d'hote*, by its songs, its shouts, its overflowing hilarity, its banner, and its alpenstocks; for since the ascension of the P. C. A. they had all supplied themselves with those mountain sticks, on which the names of celebrated climbs were inscribed, burnt in, together with popular verses.

Montreux!

Here the delegates, at the suggestion of their master, decided to halt for two or three days in order to visit the famous shores of Lake Leman, Chillon especially, and its legendary dungeon, where the great patriot Bonnivard languished, and which Byron and Delacroix have immortalized.

At heart, Tartarin cared little for Bonnivard, his adventure with William Tell having enlightened him about Swiss legends; but in passing through Interlaken he had heard that Sonia had gone to Montreux with her brother, whose health was much worse, and this invention of an historical pilgrimage was only a pretext to meet the young girl again, and, who knows? persuade her perhaps to follow him to Tarascon.

Let it be fully understood, however, that his companions believed, with the best faith in the world, that they were on their way to render homage to a great Genevese citizen whose history the P. C. A. had related to them; in fact, with their native taste for theatrical manifestations they were desirous, as soon as they landed at Montreux, of forming in line, banner displayed and marching at once to Chillon with repeated cries of "Vive Bonnivard!" The president was forced to calm them: "Breakfast first," he said, "and after that we 'll see about it." So they filled the omnibus of some Pension Mueller or other, situated, with many of its kind, close to the landing.

"*Ve!* that gendarme, how he looks at us," said Pascalon, the last to get in, with the banner, always very troublesome to install. "True," said Bravida, uneasily; "what does he want of us, that gendarme? Why does he examine us like that?"

"He recognizes me, *pardi!*" said the worthy Tartarin modestly; and he smiled upon the soldier of the Vaudois police, whose long blue hooded coat followed perseveringly behind the omnibus as it threaded its way among the poplars on the shore.

It was market-day at Montreux. Rows of little booths were open to the winds of the lake, displaying fruit, vegetables, laces very cheap, and that white jewellery, looking like manufactured snow or pearls of ice, with which the Swiss women ornament their costumes. With all this were mingled the bustle of the little port, the jostling of a whole flotilla of gayly painted pleasure-boats, the transshipment of casks and sacks from large brigantines with lateen sails, the hoarse cries, the bells of the steamers, the stir among the cafes, the breweries, the traffic of the florists and the second-hand dealers who lined the quay. If a ray of sun had fallen upon the scene, one might have thought one's self on the marina of a Mediterranean resort between Mentone and Bordighera. But sun was lacking, and the Tarasconese gazed at the pretty landscape through a watery vapour that rose from the azure lake, climbed the steep path and the pebbly little streets, and joined, above the houses, other clouds, black and gray that were clinging about the sombre verdure of the mountain, big with rain.

"***Coquin de sort!*** I'm not a lacustrian," said Spiridion Excourbanies, wiping the glass of the window to look at the perspective of glaciers and white vapours that closed the horizon in front of him...

"Nor I, either," sighed Pascalon, "this fog, this stagnant water... makes me want to cry."

Bravida complained also, in dread of his sciatic gout.

Tartarin reproved them sternly. Was it nothing to be able to relate, on their return, that they had seen the dungeon of Bonnivard, inscribed their names on its historic walls beside the signatures of Rousseau, Byron, Victor Hugo, George Sand, Eugene Sue? Suddenly, in the middle of his tirade, the president interrupted himself and changed colour... He had just caught sight of a little round hat on a coil of blond hair. Without stopping the omnibus, the pace of which had slackened in going up hill, he sprang out, calling back to the stupefied Alpinists: "Go on to the hotel..."

"Sonia!.. Sonia!.."

He feared that he might not be able to catch her, she walked so rapidly, the delicate silhouette of her shadow falling on the macadam of the road. She turned at his call and waited for him. "Ah! is it you?" she said; and as soon as they had shaken hands she walked on. He fell into step beside her, much out of breath, and began to excuse himself for having left her so abruptly... arrival of friends... necessity of making the ascension (of which his face was still bearing traces)... She listened without a word, hastening her pace, her eyes strained and fixed. Looking at her profile, she seemed to him paler, her features no longer soft with childlike innocence, but hard, a something resolute on them which till now had existed only in her voice and her imperious will; and yet her youthful grace was there, and the gold of her waving hair.

"And Boris, how is he?" asked Tartarin, rather discomfited by her silence and coldness, which began to affect him.

"Boris?.." she quivered: "Ah! true, you do not know... Well then! come, come..."

They followed a country lane leading past vineyards sloping to the lake, and villas with gardens, and elegant terraces laden with clematis, blooming with roses, petunias, and myrtles in pots. Now and then they met some foreigner with haggard cheeks and melancholy glance, walking slowly and feebly, like the many whom one meets at Mentone and Monaco; only, away down yonder the sunshine laps round all, absorbs all, while beneath this lowering cloudy sky suffering is more apparent, though the flowers seem fresher.

"Enter," said Sonia, pushing open the railed iron door of a white marble facade on which were Russian words in gilded letters.

At first Tartarin did not understand where he was. A little garden was before him with gravelled paths very carefully kept, and quantities of climbing roses hanging among the green of the trees, and bearing great clusters of white and yellow blooms, which filled the narrow space with their fragrance and glow. Among these garlands, this lovely efflorescence, a few stones were standing or lying with dates and names; the newest of which bore the words, carved on its surface:

"Boris Wassilief.
22 years."

He had been there a few days, dying almost as soon as they arrived at Montreux; and in this cemetery of foreigners the exile had found a sort of country among other Russians and Poles and Swedes, buried beneath the roses, consumptives of cold climates sent to this Northern Nice, because the Southern sun would be for them too violent, the transition too abrupt.

They stood for a moment motionless and mute before the whiteness of that new stone lying on the blackness of the fresh-turned earth; the young girl, with her head bent down, inhaling the breath of the roses, and calming, as she stood, her reddened eyes.

"Poor little girl!" said Tartarin with emotion, taking in his strong rough hands the tips of Sonia's fingers. "And you? what will you do now?"

She looked him full in the face with dry and shining eyes in which the tears no longer trembled.

"I? I leave within an hour."

"You are going?.."

"Bolibine is already in St. Petersburg... Manilof is waiting for me to cross the frontier... I return to the work. We shall be heard from." Then, in a low voice, she added with a half-smile, planting her blue glance full into that of Tartarin, which avoided it: "He who loves me follows me."

Ah! *vai*, follow her! The little fanatic frightened him. Besides, this funereal scene had cooled his love. Still, he ought not to appear to back down like a scoundrel. So, with his hand on his heart and the gesture of an Abencerrage, the hero began: "You know me, Sonia..."

She did not need to hear more.

"Gabbler!" she said, shrugging her shoulders. And she walked away, erect and proud, beneath the roses, without once turning round... Gabbler!.. not one word more, but the intonation was so contemptuous that the worthy Tartarin blushed beneath his beard, and looked about to see if they had been quite alone in the garden so that no one had overheard her.

Among our Tarasconese, fortunately, impressions do not last long. Five minutes later Tartarin was going up the terraces of Montreux with a lively step in quest of the Pension Mueller and his Alpinists, who must certainly be waiting breakfast for him; and his whole person breathed a relief, a joy at getting rid finally of that dangerous acquaintance. As he walked along he emphasized with many energetic nods the eloquent explanations which Sonia would not wait to hear, but which he gave to himself mentally: *Be!*.. yes, despotism certainly... He didn't deny that... but from that to action, *boufre!*.. And then, to make it his profession to shoot despots!.. Why, if all oppressed peoples applied to him--just as the Arabs did to Bombonnel whenever a panther roamed round their village--he couldn't suffice for them all, never!

At this moment a hired carriage coming down the hill at full speed cut short his monologue. He had scarcely time to jump upon the sidewalk with a "Take care, you brute!" when his cry of anger was changed to one of stupefaction: "*Ques aco!.. Boudiou!*.. Not possible!.."

I give you a thousand guesses to say what he saw in that old landau...

The delegation! the full delegation, Bravida, Pascalon, Excourbanies, piled upon the back seat, pale, horror-stricken, ghastly, and two gendarmes in front of them, muskets in hand! The sight of all those profiles, motionless and mute, visible through the narrow frame of the carriage window, was like a nightmare. Nailed to the ground, as formerly on the ice by his Kennedy crampons, Tartarin was gazing at that fantastic vehicle flying along at a gallop, followed at full speed by a flock of schoolboys, their atlases swinging on their backs, when a voice shouted in his ears: "And here's the fourth!.." At the same time clutched, garotted, bound, he, too, was hoisted into a *locati* with gendarmes, among them an officer armed with a gigantic cavalry sabre, which he held straight up from between his knees, the point of it touching the roof of the vehicle.

Tartarin wanted to speak, to explain. Evidently there must be some mistake... He told his name, his nation, demanded his consul, and named a seller of Swiss honey, Ichener, whom he had met at the fair at Beaucaire. Then, on the persistent silence of his captors, he bethought him that this might be another bit of machinery in Bompard's fairyland; so, addressing the officer, he said with sly air: "For fun, *que!*.. ha! *vai*, you rogue, I know very well it is all a joke."

"Not another word, or I'll gag you," said the officer, rolling terrible eyes as if he meant to spit him on his sabre.

The other kept quiet, and stirred no more, but gazed through the door at the lake, the tall mountains of a humid green, the hotels and pensions with variegated roofs and gilded signs visible for miles, and on the slopes, as at the Rigi, a coming and going of market and provision baskets, and (like the Rigi again) a comical little railway, a dangerous mechanical plaything crawling up the height to Glion, and-- to complete the resemblance to *Regina Montium*--a pouring, beating rain, an exchange of water and mist from the sky to Leman and Leman to the sky, the clouds descending till they touched the waves.

The vehicle crossed a drawbridge between a cluster of little shops of "chamoiseries," penknives, corkscrews, pocket-combs, etc., and stopped in the courtyard of an old castle overgrown with weeds, flanked by two round pepper-pot towers with black balconies guarded by parapets and supported by beams. Where was he? Tartarin learned where when he heard the officer of gendarmerie discussing the matter with the concierge of the castle, a fat man in a Greek cap who was jangling a bunch of rusty keys.

"Solitary confinement... but I haven't a place for him. The others have taken all... unless we put him in Bonnivard's dungeon."

"Yes, put him in Bonnivard's dungeon; that's good enough for him," ordered the captain; and it was done as he said.

This Castle of Chillon, about which the P. C. A. had never for two days ceased to discourse to his dear Alpinists, and in which, by the irony of fate, he found himself suddenly incarcerated without knowing why, is one of the most frequented historical monuments in Switzerland. After having served as a summer residence to the Dukes of Savoie, then as a state-prison, afterwards as an arsenal for arms and munitions, it is to-day the mere pretext for an excursion, like the Rigi and the Tellsplatte. It still contains, however, a post of gendarmerie and a "violon," that is, a cell for drunkards and the naughty boys of the neighbourhood; but they are so rare in the peaceable Canton of Vaud that the "violon" is always empty and the concierge uses it as a receptacle to store his wood for winter. Therefore the arrival of all these prisoners had put him out of temper, especially at the thought that he could no longer take visitors to see the famous dungeon, which at this season of the year is the chief profit of the place.

Furious, he showed the way to Tartarin, who followed him without the courage to make the slightest resistance. A few crumbling steps, a damp corridor smelling like a cellar, a door thick as a wall with enormous hinges, and there they were, in a vast subterranean vault, with earthen floor and heavy Roman pillars in which were still the iron rings to which prisoners of state had been chained. A dim light fell, tremulous with the shimmer of the lake, through narrow slits in the wall, which scarcely showed more than a scrap of the sky.

"Here you are at home," said the jailer. "Be careful you don't go to the farther end: the pit is there..."

Tartarin recoiled, horrified:--

"The pit! *Boudiou!*"

"What do you expect, my lad? I am ordered to put you in Bonnivard's dungeon... I have put you in Bonnivard's dungeon... Now, if you have the means, you can be furnished with certain comforts, for instance, a mattress and coverlet for the night."

"Something to eat, in the first place," said Tartarin, from whom, very luckily, they had not taken his purse.

The concierge returned with a fresh roll, beer, and a sausage, greedily devoured by the new prisoner of Chillon, fasting since the night before and hollow with fatigue and emotion. While he ate on his stone bench in the gleam of his vent-hole window, the jailer examined him with a good-natured eye.

"Faith," said he, "I don't know what you have done, nor why they should treat you so severely..."

"Nor I either, *coquin de sort!* I know nothing about it," said Tartarin, with his mouth full.

"Well, it is very certain that you don't look like a bad man, and, surely, you would n't hinder a poor father of a family from earning his living, would you?.. Now, see here!.. I have got, up above there, a whole party of people who have come to see Bonnivard's dungeon... If you would promise me to keep quiet, and not try to run away..."

The worthy Tartarin bound himself by an oath; and five minutes later he beheld his dungeon invaded by his old acquaintances on the Rigi-Kulm and the Tellsplatte, that jackass Schwan-thaler, the ineptissimus Astier-Rehu, the member of the Jockey-Club with his niece (h'm! h'm!..) and all the travellers on Cook's Circular. Ashamed, dreading to be recognized, the unfortunate man concealed himself behind pillars, getting farther and farther away as the troop of tourists advanced, preceded by the concierge and his homily, delivered in a doleful voice: "Here is where the unfortunate Bonnivard, etc..."

They advanced slowly, retarded by discussions between the two *savants*, quarrelling as usual and ready to jump at each other's throats; the one waving his campstool, the other his travelling-bag in fantastic attitudes, which the twilight from the window-slits lengthened upon the vaulted roof.

By dint of retreating, Tartarin presently found himself close to the hole of the pit, a black pit open to the level of the soil, emitting the breath of ages, malarious and glacial. Frightened, he stopped short, and curled himself into a corner, his cap over his eyes. But the damp saltpetre of the walls affected him, and suddenly a stentorian sneeze, which made the tourists recoil, gave notice of his presence.

"*Tiens*, there's Bonnivard!.." cried the bold little Parisian woman in a Directory hat whom the gentleman from the Jockey-Club called his niece.

The Tarasconese hero did not allow himself to be disconcerted.

"They are really very curious, these pits," he said, in the most natural tone in the world, as if he was visiting the dungeon, like them, for pleasure; and so saying, he mingled with the other travellers, who smiled at recognizing the Alpinist of the

Rigi-Kulm, the merry instigator of the famous ball.

"*Hi!* mossie... ballir... dantsir!.."

The comical silhouette of the little fairy Schwan-thaler rose up before him ready to seize him for a country dance. A fine mood he was in now for dancing! But not knowing how to rid himself of that determined little scrap of a woman, he offered his arm and gallantly showed her his dungeon, the ring to which the captive was chained, the trace of his steps on the stone round that pillar; and never, hearing him converse with such ease, did the good lady even dream that he too was a prisoner of state, a victim of the injustice and the wickedness of men. Terrible, however, was the departure, when the unfortunate Bonnivard, having conducted his partner to the door, took leave of her with the smile of a man of the world: "No, thank you, *vé!*.. I stay a few moments longer." Thereupon he bowed, and the jailer, who had his eye upon him, locked and bolted the door, to the stupefaction of everybody.

What a degradation! He perspired with anguish, unhappy man, while listening to the exclamations of the tourists as they walked away. Fortunately, the anguish was not renewed. No more tourists arrived that day on account of the bad weather. A terrible wind blew through the rotten boards, moans came up from the pit as from victims ill-buried, and the wash of the lake, swollen with rain, beat against the walls to the level of the window-slits and spattered its water upon the captive. At intervals the bell of a passing steamer, the clack of its paddle-wheels cut short the reflections of poor Tartarin, as evening, gray and gloomy, fell into the dungeon and seemed to enlarge it.

How explain this arrest, this imprisonment in the ill-omened place? Coste-calde, perhaps... electioneering manoeuvre at the last hour?.. Or, could it be that the Russian police, warned of his very imprudent language, his liaison with Sonia, had asked for his extradition? But if so, why arrest the delegates?.. What blame could attach to those poor unfortunates, whose terror and despair he imagined, although they were not, like him, in Bonnivard's dungeon, beneath those granite arches, where, since night had fallen, roamed monstrous rats, cockroaches, silent spiders with hairy, crooked legs.

But see what it is to possess a good conscience! In spite of rats, cold, spiders, and beetles, the great Tartarin found in the horror of that state-prison, haunted by the shades of martyrs, the same solid and sonorous sleep, mouth open, fists closed, which came to him, between the abysses and heaven, in the hut of the Alpine Club. He fancied he was dreaming when he heard his jailer say in the morning:--

"Get up; the prefect of the district is here... He has come to examine you..." Adding, with a certain respect, "To bring the prefect out in this way... why, you must be a famous scoundrel."

Scoundrel! no--but you may look like one, after spending the night in a damp and dusty dungeon without having a chance to make a toilet, however limited. And when, in the former stable of the castle transformed into a guardroom with muskets in racks along the walls,--when, I say, Tartarin, after a reassuring glance at his Alpinists seated between two gendarmes, appeared before the prefect of the district, he felt his disreputable appearance in presence of that correct and solemn magistrate with the carefully trimmed beard, who said to him sternly:--

"You call yourself Manilof, do you not?.. Russian subject... incendiary at St. Petersburg, refugee and murderer in Switzerland."

"Never in my life... It is all a mistake, an error..."

"Silence, or I 'll gag you..." interrupted the captain.

The immaculate prefect continued: "To put an end to your denials... Do you know this rope?"

His rope! *coquin de sort!* His rope, woven with iron, made at Avignon. He lowered his head, to the stupefaction of the delegates, and said: "I know it."

"With this rope a man has been hung in the Canton of Unterwald..."

Tartarin, with a shudder, swore that he had nothing to do with it.

"We shall see!"

The Italian tenor was now introduced,--in other words, the police spy whom the Nihilists had hung to the branch of an oak-tree on the Bruenig, but whose life was miraculously saved by wood-choppers.

The spy looked at Tartarin. "That is not the man," he said; then at the delegates, "Nor they, either... A mistake has been made."

The prefect, furious, turned to Tartarin. "Then, what are you doing here?" he asked.

"That is what I ask myself, *ve!*.." replied the president, with the aplomb of innocence.

After a short explanation the Alpinists of Tarascon, restored to liberty, departed from the Castle of Chillon, where none have ever felt its oppressive and romantic melancholy more than they. They stopped at the Pension Mueller to get their luggage and banner, and to pay for the breakfast of the day before which they had not had time to eat; then they started for Geneva by the train. It rained. Through the streaming windows they read the names of stations of aristocratic villeggiatura: Clarens, Vevey, Lausanne; red chalets, little gardens of rare shrubs passed them under a misty veil, the branches of the trees, the turrets on the roofs, the galleries of the hotels all dripping.

Installed in one corner of a long railway carriage, on two seats facing each other, the Alpinists had a downcast and discomfited appearance. Bravida, very sour, complained of aches, and repeatedly asked Tartarin with savage irony: "Eh *be!*you've seen it now, that dungeon of Bonnivard's that you were so set on seeing... I think you have seen it, *que?*" Excourbanies, voiceless for the first time in his life, gazed piteously at the lake which escorted them the whole way: "Water! more water, *Boudiou!*.. after this, I 'll never in my life take another bath."

Stupefied by a terror which still lasts, Pascalon, the banner between his legs, sat back in his seat, looking to right and left like a hare fearful of being caught again... And Tartarin?.. Oh! he, ever dignified and calm, he was diverting himself by reading the Southern newspapers, a package of which had been sent to the Pension Mueller, all of them having reproduced from the *Forum* the account of his ascension, the same he had himself dictated, but enlarged, magnified, and embellished with ineffable laudations. Suddenly the hero gave a cry, a formidable cry, which resounded to the end of the carriage. All the travellers sat up excitedly, expecting an accident. It was simply an item in the *Forum*, which Tartarin now read to his Alpinists:--

"Listen to this: 'Rumour has it that V. P. C. A. Costecalde, though scarcely recovered from the jaundice which kept him in bed for some days, is about to start for the ascension of Mont Blanc; to climb higher than Tartarin!..' Oh! the villain... He wants to ruin the effect of my Jung-frau... Well, well! wait a bit; I 'll blow you out of water, you and your mountain... Chamounix is only a few hours from Geneva; I'll do Mont Blanc before him! Will you come, my children?"

Bravida protested. *Outre!* he had had enough of adventures.

"Enough and more than enough..." howled Excourbanies, in his almost extinct voice.

"And you, Pascalon?" asked Tartarin, gently.

The pupil dared not raise his eyes:--

"Ma-a-aster..." He, too, abandoned him!

"Very good," said the hero, solemnly and angrily. "I will go alone; all the honour will be mine... ***Zou!*** give me back the banner..."

XII.

Hotel Baltet at Chamonix. "I smell garlic!" The use of rope
in Alpine climbing. "Shake hands." A pupil of Schopenhauer.
At the hut on the Grands-Mulets. "Tartarin, I must speak to
you."

Nine o'clock was ringing from the belfry at Chamonix of a cold night shivering with the north wind and rain; the black streets, the darkened houses (except, here and there, the facades and courtyards of hotels where the gas was still burning) made the surroundings still more gloomy under the vague reflection of the snow of the mountains, white as a planet on the night of the sky.

At the Hotel Baltet, one of the best and most frequented inns of this Alpine village, the numerous travellers and boarders had disappeared one by one, weary with the excursions of the day, until no one was left in the grand salon but one English traveller playing silently at backgammon with his wife, his innumerable daughters, in brown-holland aprons with bibs, engaged in copying notices of an approaching evangelical service, and a young Swede sitting before the fireplace, in which was a good fire of blazing logs. The latter was pale, hollow-cheeked, and gazed at the flame with a gloomy air as he drank his grog of kirsch and seltzer. From time to time some belated traveller crossed the salon, with soaked gaiters and streaming mackintosh, looked at the great barometer hanging to the wall, tapped it, consulted the mercury as to the weather of the following day, and went off to bed in consternation. Not a word; no other manifestations of life than the crackling of the fire, the pattering on the panes, and the angry roll of the Arve under the arches of its wooden bridge, a few yards distant from the hotel.

Suddenly the door of the salon opened, a porter in a silver-laced coat came in, carrying valises and rugs, with four shivering Alpinists behind him, dazzled by the sudden change from icy darkness into warmth and light.

"***Boudiou!*** what weather!.."

"Something to eat, ***zou!***"

"Warm the beds, ***que!***"

They all talked at once from the depths of their mufflers and ear-pads, and it was hard to know which to obey, when a short stout man, whom the others called "***presidain***" enforced silence by shouting more loudly than they.

"In the first place, give me the visitors' book," he ordered. Turning it over with a numbed hand, he read aloud the names of all who had been at the hotel for the last week: "'Doctor Schwanthaler and madame.' Again!.. 'Astier-Rehu of the French Academy...'" He deciphered thus two or three pages, turning pale when he thought he saw the name he was in search of. Then, at the end, flinging the book on the table with a laugh of triumph, the squat man made a boyish gambol quite extraordinary in one of his bulky shape: "He is not here, ***ve!*** he has n't come... And yet he must have stopped here if he had... Done for! Coste-calde... lagadigadeou!.. quick! to our suppers, children!.. "And the worthy Tartarin, having bowed to the ladies, marched to the dining-room, followed by the famished and tumultuous delegation.

Ah, yes! the delegation, all of them, even Bravida himself... Is it possible? come now!.. But--just think what would be said of them down there in Tarascon, if they returned without Tartarin? They each felt this. And, at the moment of separation in the station at Geneva, the buffet witnessed a pathetic scene of tears, embraces, heartrending adieus to the banner; as the result of which adieus the whole company piled itself into the landau which Tartarin had chartered to take him to Chamonix. A glorious route, which they did with their eyes shut, wrapped in their rugs and filling the carriage with sonorous snores, unmindful of the wonderful landscape, which, from Sallanches, was unrolling before them in a mist of blue rain: ravines, forests, foaming waterfalls, with the crest of Mont Blanc above the clouds, visible or vanishing, according to the lay of the land in the valley they were crossing. Tired of that sort of natural beauty, our Tarasconese friends thought only of making up for the wretched night they had spent behind the bolts of Chillon. And even now, at the farther end of the long, deserted dining-room of the Hotel Baltet, when served with the warmed-over soup and *entrees* of the **table d'hote**, they ate voraciously, without saying a word, eager only to get to bed. All of a sudden, Excourbanies, who was swallowing his food like a somnambulist, came out of his plate, and sniffing the air about him, remarked: "I smell garlic!.."

"True, I smell it," said Bravida. And the whole party, revived by this reminder of home, these fumes of the national dishes, which Tartarin, at least, had not inhaled for so long, turned round in their chairs with gluttonous anxiety. The odour came from the other end of the dining-room, from a little room where some one was supping apart, a personage of importance, no doubt, for the white cap of the head cook was constantly appearing at the wicket that opened into the kitchen as he passed to the girl in waiting certain little covered dishes which she conveyed to the inner apartment.

"Some one from the South, that's certain," murmured the gentle Pascalon; and the president, becoming ghastly at the idea of Costecalde, said commandingly:--

"Go and see, Spiridion... and bring us word who it is..."

A loud roar of laughter came from that little apartment as soon as the brave "gong" entered it, at the order of his chief; and he presently returned, leading by the hand a tall devil with a big nose, a mischievous eye, and a napkin under his chin, like the gastronomic horse.

"*Vi!* Bompard..."

"*Te!* the Impostor..."

"*He!* Gonzague... How are you?"

"*Differemment*, messieurs: your most obedient..." said the courier, shaking hands with all, and sitting down at the table of the Tarasconese to share with them a dish of mushrooms with garlic prepared by *mere* Baltet, who, together with her husband had a horror of the cooking for the **table d'hote**.

Was it the national concoction, or the joy of meeting a compatriot, that delightful Bompard with his inexhaustible imagination? Certain it is that weariness and the desire to sleep took wings, champagne was uncorked, and, with moustachios all messy with froth, they laughed and shouted and gesticulated, clasping one another round the body effusively happy.

"I'll not leave you now, *ve!*" said Bompard. "My Peruvians have gone... I am free..."

"Free!.. Then to-morrow you and I will ascend Mont Blanc."

"Ah! you do Mont Blanc to-morrow?" said Bompard, without enthusiasm.

"Yes, I knock out Costecalde... When he gets here, *uit!*.. No Mont Blanc for him... You'll go, *que*, Gonzague?"

"I 'll go... I 'll go... that is, if the weather permits... The fact is, that the mountain is not always suitable at this season."

"Ah! *vai*! not suitable indeed!.." exclaimed Tartarin, crinkling up his eyes by a meaning laugh which Bompard seemed not to understand.

"Let us go into the salon for our coffee... We 'll consult *pere* Baltet. He knows all about it, he 's an old guide who has made the ascension twenty-seven times."

All the delegates cried out: "Twenty-seven times! *Boufre!*"

"Bompard always exaggerates," said the P. C. A. severely, but not without a touch of envy.

In the salon they found the daughters of the minister still bending over their notices, while the father and mother were asleep at their backgammon, and the tall Swede was stirring his seltzer grog with the same disheartened gesture. But the invasion of the Tarasconese Alpinists, warmed by champagne, caused, as may well be supposed, some distraction of mind to the young conventiclers. Never had those charming young persons seen coffee taken with such rollings of the eyes and pantomimic action.

"Sugar, Tartarin?"

"Of course not, commander... You know very well... Since Africa!.."

"True; excuse me... *Te!* here comes M. Baltet."

"Sit down there, *que*. Monsieur Baltet."

"Vive Monsieur Baltet!.. Ha! ha! *fen de brut*."

Surrounded, captured by all these men whom he had never seen before in his life, *pere* Baltet smiled with a tranquil air. A robust Savoyard, tall and broad, with a round back and slow walk, a heavy face, close-shaven, enlivened by two shrewd eyes, that were still young, contrasting oddly with his baldness, caused by chills at dawn upon the mountain.

"These gentlemen wish to ascend Mont Blanc?" he said, gauging the Tarasconese Alpinists with a glance both humble and sarcastic. Tartarin was about to reply, but Bompard forestalled him:-- "Isn't the season too far advanced?" "Why, no," replied the former guide. "Here's a Swedish gentleman who goes up to-morrow, and I am expecting at the end of this week two American gentlemen to make the ascent; and one of them is blind."

"I know. I met them on the Guggi." "Ah! monsieur has been upon the Guggi?" "Yes, a week ago, in doing the Jungfrau." Here a quiver among the evangelical conventiclers; all pens stopped, and heads were raised in the direction of Tartarin, who, to the eyes of these English maidens, resolute climbers, expert in all sports, acquired considerable authority. He had gone up the Jungfrau!

"A fine thing!" said *pere* Baltet, considering the P. C. A. with some astonishment; while Pascalon, intimidated by the ladies and blushing and stuttering, murmured softly:--

"Ma-a-aster, tell them the... the... thing... crevasse."

The president smiled. "Child!.." he said: but, all the same, he began the tale of his fall; first with a careless, indifferent air, and then with startled motions, jigglings at the end of the rope over the abyss, hands outstretched and appealing. The young ladies quivered, and devoured him with those cold English eyes, those eyes that open round.

In the silence that followed, rose the voice of Bompard:--

"On Chimborazo we never roped one another to cross crevasses."

The delegates looked at one another. As a tarasconade that remark surpassed them all.

"Oh, *that* Bompard, *pas mouain*..." murmured Pascalon, with ingenuous admiration.

But pere Baltet, taking Chimborazo seriously, protested against the practice of not roping. According to him, no ascension over ice was possible without a rope, a good rope of Manila hemp; then, if one slipped, the others could hold him.

"Unless the rope breaks, Monsieur Baltet," said Tartarin, remembering the catastrophe on the Matterhorn.

But the landlord, weighing his words, replied:

"The rope did not break on the Matterhorn... the rear guide cut it with a blow of his axe..."

As Tartarin expressed indignation,--

"Beg pardon, monsieur, but the guide had a right to do it... He saw the impossibility of holding back those who had fallen, and he detached himself from them to save his life, that of his son, and of the traveller they were accompanying... Without his action seven persons would have lost their lives instead of four."

Then a discussion began. Tartarin thought that in letting yourself be roped in file you were bound in honour to live and die together; and growing excited, especially in presence of ladies, he backed his opinion by facts and by persons present: "Tomorrow, *te!* to-morrow, in roping myself to Bom-pard, it is not a simple precaution that I shall take, it is an oath before God and man to be one with my companion and to die sooner than return without him, *coquin de sort!*"

"I accept the oath for myself, as for you, Tar-tarin..." cried Bompard from the other side of the round table.

Exciting moment!

The minister, electrified, rose, came to the hero and inflicted upon him a pump-handle exercise of the hand that was truly English. His wife did likewise, then all the young ladies continued the *shake hands* with enough vigour to have brought water to the fifth floor of the house. The delegates, I ought to mention, were less enthusiastic.

"Eh, *be!* as for me," said Bravida, "I am of M. Baltet's opinion. In matters of this kind, each man should look to his own skin, *pardi!* and I understand that cut of the axe perfectly."

"You amaze me, Placide," said Tartarin, severely; adding in a low voice: "Behave yourself! England is watching us."

The old captain, who certainly had kept a root of bitterness in his heart ever since the excursion to Chillon, made a gesture that signified: "I don't care *that* for England..." and might perhaps have drawn upon himself a sharp rebuke from the president, irritated at so much cynicism, but at this moment the young man with the heart-broken look, filled to the full with grog and melancholy, brought his extremely bad French into the conversation. He thought, he said, that the guide was right to cut the rope: to deliver from existence those four unfortunate men, still young, condemned to live for many years longer; to send them, by a mere gesture, to peace, to nothingness,--what a noble and generous action!

Tartarin exclaimed against it:--

"Pooh! young man, at your age, to talk of life with such aversion, such anger... What has life done to you?"

"Nothing; it bores me." He had studied philosophy at Christiania, and since then, won to the ideas of Schopenhauer and Hartmann, he had found existence dreary, inept, chaotic. On the verge of suicide he shut his books, at the entreaty of his parents, and started to travel, striking everywhere against the same distress, the gloomy wretchedness of this life. Tartarin and his friends, he said, seemed to him the only beings content to live that he had ever met with.

The worthy P. C. A. began to laugh. "It is all race, young man. Everybody feels like that in Tarascon. That's the land of the good God. From morning till night we laugh and sing, and the rest of the time we dance the farandole... like this... *te!*" So saying, he cut a double shuffle with the grace and lightness of a big cockchafer trying its wings.

But the delegates had not the steel nerves nor the indefatigable spirit of their chief. Excour-banies growled out: "He 'll keep us here till midnight." But Bravida jumped up, furious. "Let us go to bed, *ve!* I can't stand my sciatica..." Tartarin consented, remembering the ascension on the morrow; and the Tarasconese, candlesticks in hand, went up the broad staircase of granite that led to the chambers, while Baltet went to see about provisions and hire the mules and guides.

"*Te!* it is snowing..."

Those were the first words of the worthy Tartarin when he woke in the morning and saw his windows covered with frost and his bedroom inundated with white reflections. But when he hooked his little mirror as usual to the window-fastening, he understood his mistake, and saw that Mont Blanc, sparkling before him in the splendid sunshine, was the cause of that light. He opened his window to the breeze of the glacier, keen and refreshing, bringing with it the sound of the cattle-bells as the herds followed the long, lowing sound of the shepherd's horn. Something fortifying, pastoral, filled the atmosphere such as he had never before breathed in Switzerland.

Below, an assemblage of guides and porters awaited him. The Swede was already mounted upon his mule, and among the spectators, who formed a circle, was the minister's family, all those active young ladies, their hair in early morning style, who had come for another "shake hands" with the hero who had haunted their dreams.

"Splendid weather! make haste!.." cried the landlord, whose skull was gleam-
ing in the sunshine like a pebble. But though Tartarin himself might hasten, it was
not so easy a matter to rouse from sleep his dear Alpinists, who intended to accompany him as far as the Pierre-Pointue, where the mule-path ends. Neither prayers
nor arguments could persuade the Commander to get out of bed. With his cotton
nightcap over his ears and his face to the wall, he contented himself with replying
to Tartarin's objurgations by a cynical Tarasconese proverb: "Whoso has the credit
of getting up early may sleep until midday..." As for Bom-pard, he kept repeating,
the whole time, "Ah, *vai*, Mont Blanc... what a humbug..." Nor did they rise until
the P. C. A. had issued a formal order.

At last, however, the caravan started, and passed through the little streets in
very imposing array: Pascalon on the leading mule, banner unfurled; and last in
file, grave as a mandarin amid the guides and porters on either side his mule, came
the worthy Tartarin, more stupendously Alpinist than ever, wearing a pair of new
spectacles with smoked and convex glasses, and his famous rope made at Avignon,
recovered--we know at what cost.

Very much looked at, almost as much as the banner, he was jubilant under his
dignified mask, enjoyed the picturesqueness of these Savoyard village streets, so
different from the too neat, too varnished Swiss village, looking like a new toy; he
enjoyed the contrast of these hovels scarcely rising above the ground, where the
stable fills the largest space, with the grand and sumptuous hotels five storeys high,
the glittering signs of which were as much out of keeping with the hovels as the
gold-laced cap of the porter and the pumps and black coats of the waiters with the
Savoyard head-gear, the fustian jackets, the felt hats of the charcoal-burners with
their broad wings.

On the square were landaus with the horses taken out, manure-carts side by
side with travelling-carriages, and a troop of pigs idling in the sun before the post-
office, from which issued an Englishman in a white linen cap, with a package of letters and a copy of ***The Times***, which he read as he walked along, before he opened
his correspondence. The cavalcade of the Tarasconese passed all this, accompanied
by the scuffling of mules, the war-cry of Excourbanies (to whom the sun had restored the use of his gong), the pastoral chimes on the neighbouring slopes, and the

dash of the river, gushing from the glacier in a torrent all white and sparkling, as if it bore upon its breast both sun and snow.

On leaving the village Bompard rode his mule beside that of the president, and said to the latter; rolling his eyes in a most extraordinary manner: "Tartarin, I **must** speak to you..."

"Presently..." said the P. C. A., then engaged in a philosophical discussion with the young Swede, whose black pessimism he was endeavouring to correct by the marvellous spectacle around them, those pastures with great zones of light and shade, those forests of sombre green crested with the whiteness of the dazzling **neves**.

After two attempts to speak to the president, Bompard was forced to give it up. The Arve having been crossed by a little bridge, the caravan now entered one of those narrow, zigzag roads among the firs where the mules, one by one, follow with their fantastic sabots all the sinuosities of the ravines, and our tourists had their attention fully occupied in keeping their equilibrium by the help of many an "**Outre!.. Boufre!**.. gently, gently!.." with which they guided their beasts.

At the chalet of the Pierre-Pointue, where Pas-calon and Excourbanies were to wait the return of the excursionists, Tartarin, much occupied in ordering breakfast and in looking after porters and guides, still paid no attention to Bompard's whisperings. But--singular fact, which was not remarked until later--in spite of the fine weather, the good wine, and that purified atmosphere of ten thousand feet above sea-level, the breakfast was melancholy. While they heard the guides laughing and making merry apart, the table of the Taras-conese was silent except for the rattle of glasses and the clatter of the heavy plates and covers on the white wood. Was it the presence of that morose Swede, or the visible uneasiness of Bompard, or some presentiment? At any rate, the party set forth, sad as a battalion without its band, towards the glacier of the Bossons, where the true ascent begins.

On setting foot upon the ice, Tartarin could not help smiling at the recollection of the Guggi and his perfected crampons. What a difference between the neophyte he then was and the first-class Alpinist he felt he had become! Steady on his heavy boots, which the porter of the hotel had ironed that very morning with four stout nails, expert in wielding his ice-axe, he scarcely needed the hand of a guide, and then less to support him than to show him the way. The smoked glasses moderated the reflections of the glacier, which a recent avalanche had powdered with fresh snow, and through which little spaces of a glaucous green showed themselves here and there, slippery and treacherous. Very calm, confident through experience that there was not the slightest danger, Tartarin walked along the verge of the crevasses with their smooth, iridescent sides stretching downward indefinitely, and made his way among the *seracs*, solely intent on keeping up with the Swedish student, an intrepid walker, whose long gaiters with their silver buckles marched, thin and lank, beside his alpenstock, which looked like a third leg. Their philosophical discussion continuing, in spite of the difficulties of the way, a good stout voice, familiar and panting, could be heard in the frozen space, sonorous as the swell of a river: "You know me, Otto..."

Bompard all this time was undergoing misadventures. Firmly convinced, up to that very morning, that Tartarin would never go to the length of his vaunting, and would no more ascend Mont Blanc than he had the Jungfrau, the luckless courier had dressed himself as usual, without nailing his boots, or even utilizing his famous invention for shoeing the feet of soldiers, and without so much as his alpenstock, the mountaineers of the Chimborazo never using them. Armed only with a little switch, quite in keeping with the blue ribbon of his hat and his ulster, this approach to the glacier terrified him, for, in spite of his tales, it is, of course, well understood that the Impostor had never in his life made an ascension. He was somewhat reassured, however, on seeing from the top of the moraine with what facility Tartarin made his way on the ice; and he resolved to follow him as far as the hut on the Grands-Mulets, where it was intended to pass the night. He did not get there without difficulty. His first step laid him flat on his back; at the second he fell forward on his hands and knees: "No, thank you, I did it on purpose," he said to the guides who endeavoured to pick him up. "American fashion, *ve!*.. as they do on the Chimborazo." That position seeming to be convenient, he kept it, creeping on four paws, his hat pushed back, and his ulster sweeping the ice like the pelt of a gray bear; very calm, withal, and relating to those about him that in the Cordilleras of the Andes he had scaled a mountain thirty thousand feet high. He did not say how much time it took him, but it must have been long, judging by this stage to the Grands-Mulets, where he arrived an hour after Tartarin, a disgusting mass of muddy snow, with frozen hands in his knitted gloves.

In comparison with the hut on the Guggi, that which the commune of Chamonix has built on the Grands-Mulets is really comfortable. When Bompard entered the kitchen, where a grand wood-fire was blazing, he found Tartarin and the Swedish student drying their boots, while the hut-keeper, a shrivelled old fellow with long white hair that fell in meshes, exhibited the treasures of his little museum.

Of evil augury, this museum is a reminder of all the catastrophes known to have taken place on the Mont Blanc for the forty years that the old man had kept the inn, and as he took them from their show-case, he related the lamentable origin of each of them... This piece of cloth and those waistcoat buttons were the memorial of a Russian *savant*, hurled by a hurricane upon the Brenva glacier... These jaw teeth were all that remained of one of the guides of a famous caravan of eleven travellers and porters who disappeared forever in a *tourmente* of snow... In the fading light and the pale reflection of the *neves* against the window, the production of these mortuary relics, these monotonous recitals, had something very poignant about them, and all the more because the old man softened his quavering voice at pathetic items, and even shed tears on displaying a scrap of green veil worn by an English lady rolled down by an avalanche in 1827.

In vain Tartarin reassured himself by dates, convinced that in those early days the Company had not yet organized the ascensions without danger; this Savoyard *vocero* oppressed his heart, and he went to the doorway for a moment to breathe.

Night had fallen, engulfing the depths. The Bossons stood out, livid, and very close; while the Mont Blanc reared its summit, still rosy, still caressed by the departed sun. The Southerner was recovering his serenity from this smile of nature when the shadow of Bompard rose behind him.

"Is that you, Gonzague... As you see, I am getting the good of the air... He annoyed me, that old fellow, with his stories."

"Tartarin," said Bompard, squeezing the arm of the P. C. A. till he nearly ground it, "I hope that this is enough, and that you are going to put an end to this ridiculous expedition."

The great man opened wide a pair of astonished eyes.

"What stuff are you talking to me now?"

Whereupon Bompard made a terrible picture of the thousand deaths that awaited him; crevasses, avalanches, hurricanes, whirlwinds...

Tartarin interrupted him:--

"Ah! *vai*, you rogue; and the Company? Isn't Mont Blanc managed like the rest?"

"Managed?. the Company?.." said Bompard, bewildered, remembering nothing whatever of his tarasconade, which Tartarin now repeated to him word for word-- Switzerland a vast Association, lease of the mountains, machinery of the crevasses; on which the former courier burst out laughing.

"What! you really believed me?.. Why, that was a *galejade* a fib... Among us Taras-conese you ought surely to know what talking means..."

"Then," asked Tartarin, with much emotion, "the Jungfrau was not *pre-pared?*"

"Of course not."

"And if the rope had broken?.."

"Ah! my poor friend..."

The hero closed his eyes, pale with retrospective terror, and for one moment he hesitated... This landscape of polar cataclysm, cold, gloomy, yawning with gulfs... those laments of the old hut-man still weeping in his ears... *Outre!* what will they make me do?.. Then, suddenly, he thought of the *folk* at Tarascon, of the banner to be unfurled "up there," and he said to himself that with good guides and a trusty companion like Bompard... He had done the Jungfrau... why should n't he do Mont Blanc?

Laying his large hand on the shoulder of his friend, he began in a virile voice:--

"Listen to me, Gonzague..."

XIII.

The catastrophe.

On a dark, dark night, moonless, starless, skyless, on the trembling whiteness of a vast ledge of snow, slowly a long rope unrolled itself, to which were attached in file certain timorous and very small shades, preceded, at the distance of a hundred feet, by a lantern casting a red light along the way. Blows of an ice-axe ringing on the hard snow, the roll of the ice blocks thus detached, alone broke the silence of the *neve* on which the steps of the caravan made no sound. From minute to minute, a cry, a smothered groan, the fall of a body on the ice, and then immediately a strong voice sounding from the end of the rope: "Go gently, Gonzague, and don't fall." For poor Bompard had made up his mind to follow his friend Tartarin to the summit of Mont Blanc. Since two in the morning--it was now four by the president's repeater--the hapless courier had groped along, a galley slave on the chain, dragged, pushed, vacillating, balking, compelled to restrain the varied exclamations extorted from him by his mishaps, for an avalanche was on the watch, and the slightest concussion, a mere vibration of the crystalline air, might send down its masses of snow and ice. To suffer in silence! what torture to a native of Tarascon!

But the caravan halted. Tartarin asked why. A discussion in low voice was heard; animated whisperings: "It is your companion who won't come on," said the Swedish student. The order of march was broken; the human chaplet returned upon itself, and they found themselves all at the edge of a vast crevasse, called by the mountaineers a *roture*. Preceding ones they had crossed by means of a ladder, over which they crawled on their hands and knees; here the crevasse was much wider and the ice-cliff rose on the other side to a height of eighty or a hundred feet. It was necessary to descend to the bottom of the gully, which grew smaller as it went down, by means of steps cut in the ice, and to reascend in the same way on the other side. But Bompard obstinately refused to do so.

Leaning over the abyss, which the shadows represented as bottomless, he watched through the damp vapour the movements of the little lantern by which the guides below were preparing the way. Tartarin, none too easy himself, warmed his own courage by exhorting his friend: "Come now, Gonzague, *zou!*" and then in a lower voice coaxed him to honour, invoked the banner, Tarascon, the Club...

"Ah! *vai*, the Club indeed!.. I don't belong to it," replied the other, cynically.

Then Tartarin explained to him where to set his feet, and assured him that nothing was easier.

"For you, perhaps, but not for me..." "But you said you had a habit of it..." "*Be!* yes! habit, of course... which habit? I have so many... habit of smoking, sleeping..."

"And lying, especially," interrupted the president.

"Exaggerating--come now!" said Bompard, not the least in the world annoyed.

However, after much hesitation, the threat of leaving him there all alone decided him to go slowly, deliberately, down that terrible miller's ladder... The going up was more difficult, for the other face was nearly perpendicular, smooth as marble, and higher than King Rene's tower at Tarascon. From below, the winking light of the guides going up, looked like a glow-worm on the march. He was forced to follow, however, for the snow beneath his feet was not solid, and gurgling sounds of circulating water heard round a fissure told of more than could be seen at the foot of that wall of ice, of depths that were sending upward the chilling breath of subterranean abysses.

"Go gently, Gonzague, for fear of falling..." That phrase, which Tartarin uttered with tender intonations, almost supplicating, borrowed a solemn signification from the respective positions of the ascensionists, clinging with feet and hands one above the other to the wall, bound by the rope and the similarity of their movements, so that the fall or the awkwardness of one put all in danger. And what danger! *coquin de sort!* It sufficed to hear fragments of the ice-wall bounding and dashing downward with the echo of their fall to imagine the open jaws of the monster watching there below to snap you up at the least false step.

But what is this?.. Lo, the tall Swede, next above Tartarin, has stopped and touches with his iron heels the cap of the P. C. A. In vain the guides called: "Forward!.." And the president: "Go on, young man!.." He did not stir. Stretched at full length, clinging to the ice with careless hand, the Swede leaned down, the glimmering dawn touching his scanty beard and giving light to the singular expression of his dilated eyes, while he made a sign to Tartarin:--

"What a fall, hey? if one let go..."

"*Outre!* I should say so... you would drag us all down... Go on!"

The other remained motionless.

"A fine chance to be done with life, to return into chaos through the bowels of the earth, and roll from fissure to fissure like that bit of ice which I kick with my foot..." And he leaned over frightfully to watch the fragment bounding downward and echoing endlessly in the blackness.

"Take care!.." cried Tartarin, livid with terror. Then, desperately clinging to the

oozing wall, he resumed, with hot ardour, his argument of the night before in fa-
vour of existence. "There's ***good*** in it... What the deuce!.. At your age, a fine young
fellow like you... Don't you believe in love, ***que!***"

No, the Swede did not believe in it. Ideal love is a poet's lie; the other, only a
need he had never felt...

"***Be!*** yes! ***be!*** yes!.. It is true poets lie, they always say more than there is; but
for all that, she is nice, the ***femellan***--that's what they call women in our parts.
Besides, there's children, pretty little darlings that look like us."

"Children! a source of grief. Ever since she had them my mother has done
nothing but weep."

"Listen, Otto, you know me, my good friend..."

And with all the valorous ardour of his soul Tartarin exhausted himself to re-
vive and rub to life at that distance this victim of Schopenhauer and of Hartmann,
two rascals he'd like to catch at the corner of a wood, ***coquin de sort!*** and make
them pay for all the harm they had done to youth...

Represent to yourselves during this discussion the high wall of freezing, glaucous, streaming ice touched by a pallid ray of light, and that string of human beings
glued to it in echelon, with ill-omened rumblings rising from the yawning depth,
together with the curses of the guides and their threats to detach and abandon
the travellers. Tartarin, seeing that no argument could convince the madman or
clear off his vertigo of death, suggested to him the idea of throwing himself from
the highest peak of the Mont Blanc... That indeed! ***that*** would be worth doing, up
there! A fine end among the elements... But here, at the bottom of a cave... Ah! ***vai***,
what a blunder!.. And he put such tone into his words, brusque and yet persuasive,
such conviction, that the Swede allowed himself to be conquered, and there they
were, at last, one by one, at the top of that terrible ***roture***.

They were now unroped, and a halt was called for a bite and sup. It was daylight; a cold wan light among a circle of peaks and shafts, overtopped by the Mont
Blanc, still thousands of feet above them. The guides were apart, gesticulating and
consulting, with many shakings of the head. Seated on the white ground, heavy
and huddled up, their round backs in their brown jackets, they looked like marmots
getting ready to hibernate. Bompard and Tartarin, uneasy, shocked, left the young
Swede to eat alone, and came up to the guides just as their leader was saying with

a grave air:--

"He is smoking his pipe; there's no denying it."

"Who is smoking his pipe?" asked Tartarin.

"Mont Blanc, monsieur; look there..."

And the guide pointed to the extreme top of the highest peak, where, like a plume, a white vapour floated toward Italy.

"*Et autremain*, my good friend, when the Mont Blanc smokes his pipe, what does that mean?"

"It means, monsieur, that there is a terrible wind on the summit, and a snow-storm which will be down upon us before long. And I tell you, that's dangerous."

"Let us go back," said Bompard, turning green; and Tartarin added:--

"Yes, yes, certainly; no false vanity, of course."

But here the Swedish student interfered. He had paid his money to be taken to the top of Mont Blanc, and nothing should prevent his getting there. He would go alone, if no one would accompany him. "Cowards! cowards!" he added, turning to the guides; and he uttered the insult in the same ghostly voice with which he had roused himself just before to suicide.

"You shall see if we are cowards... Fasten to the rope and forward!" cried the head guide. This time, it was Bompard who protested energetically. He had had enough, and he wanted to be taken back. Tartarin supported him vigorously.

"You see very well that that young man is insane..." he said, pointing to the Swede, who had already started with great strides through the heavy snow-flakes which the wind was beginning to whirl on all sides. But nothing could stop the men who had just been called cowards. The marmots were now wide-awake and heroic. Tartarin could not even obtain a conductor to take him back with Bompard to the Grands-Mulets. Besides, the way was very easy; three hours' march, count-ing a detour of twenty minutes to get round that *roture*, if they were afraid to go through it alone.

"*Outre!* yes, we are afraid of it..." said Bompard, without the slightest shame; and the two parties separated.

Bompard and the P. C. A. were now alone. They advanced with caution on the snowy desert, fastened to a rope: Tartarin first, feeling his way gravely with his ice-axe; filled with a sense of responsibility and finding relief in it.

"Courage! keep cool!.. We shall get out of it all right," he called to Bompard repeatedly. It is thus that an officer in battle, seeking to drive away his own fear, brandishes his sword and shouts to his men: "Forward! *s. n. de D*!.. all balls don't kill."

At last, here they were at the end of that horrible crevasse. From there to the hut there were no great obstacles; but the wind blew, and blinded them with snowy whirlwinds. Further advance was impossible for fear of losing their way.

"Let us stop here for a moment," said Tartarin. A gigantic *serac* of ice offered them a hollow at its base. Into it they crept, spreading down the india-rubber rug of the president and opening a flask of rum, the sole article of provision left them by the guides. A little warmth and comfort followed thereon, while the blows of the ice-axes, getting fainter and fainter up the height, told them of the progress of the expedition. They echoed in the heart of the P. C. A. like a pang of regret for not having done the Mont Blanc to the summit.

"Who 'll know it?" returned Bompard, cynically. "The porters kept the banner, and Chamonix will believe it is you."

"You are right," cried Tartarin, in a tone of conviction; "the honour of Tarascon is safe..."

But the elements grew furious, the north-wind a hurricane, the snow flew in volumes. Both were silent, haunted by sinister ideas; they remembered those ill-omened relics in the glass case of the old inn-keeper, his laments, the legend of that American tourist found petrified with cold and hunger, holding in his stiffened hand a note-book, in which his agonies were written down even to the last convulsion, which made the pencil slip and the signature uneven.

"Have you a note-book, Gonzague?"

And the other, comprehending without further explanation:--

"Ha! *vai*, a note-book!.. If you think I am going to let myself die like that American!.. Quick, let's get on! come out of this."

"Impossible... At the first step we should be blown like straws and pitched into some abyss."

"Well then, we had better shout; the Grands-Mulets is not far off..." And Bompard, on his knees, in the attitude of a cow at pasture, lowing, roared out, "Help! help! help!.."

"To arms!" shouted Tartarin, in his most sonorous chest voice, which the grotto repercussioned in thunder.

Bompard seized his arm: "Horrors! the *serac!*.. Positively the whole block was trembling; another shout and that mass of accumulated icicles would be down upon their heads. They stopped, rigid, motionless, wrapped in a horrid silence, presently broken by a distant rolling sound, coming nearer, increasing, spreading to the horizon, and dying at last far down, from gulf to gulf.

"Poor souls!" murmured Tartarin, thinking of the Swede and his guides caught, no doubt, and swept away by the avalanche.

Bompard shook his head: "We are scarcely better off than they," he said.

And truly, their situation was alarming; but they did not dare to stir from their icy grotto, nor to risk even their heads outside in the squall.

To complete the oppression of their hearts, from the depths of the valley rose the howling of a dog, baying at death. Suddenly Tartarin, with swollen eyes, his lips quivering, grasped the hands of his companion, and looking at him gently, said:--

"Forgive me, Gonzague, yes, yes, forgive me. I was rough to you just now; I treated you as a liar..."

"Ah! *vai*. What harm did that do me?"

"I had less right than any man to do so, for I have lied a great deal myself, and at this supreme moment I feel the need to open my heart, to free my bosom, to publicly confess my imposture..."

"Imposture, you?"

"Listen to me, my friend... In the first place, I never killed a lion."

"I am not surprised at that," said Bompard, composedly. "But why do you worry yourself for such a trifle?.. It is our sun that does it... we are born to lies... *Ve!* look at me... Did I ever tell the truth since I came into the world? As soon as I open my mouth my South gets up into my head like a fit. The people I talk about I never knew; the countries, I 've never set foot in them; and all that makes such a tissue of inventions that I can't unravel it myself any longer."

"That's imagination, *pechere!*" sighed Tartarin; "we are liars of imagination."

"And such lies never do any harm to any one; whereas a malicious, envious man, like Coste-calde..."

"Don't ever speak to me of that wretch," interrupted the P. C. A.; then, seized with a sudden attack of wrath, he shouted: "***Coquin de bon sorti*** it is, all the same, rather vexing..." He stopped, at a terrified gesture from Bompard, "Ah! yes, true... the ***serac***;" and, forced to lower his tone and mutter his rage, poor Tartarin continued his imprecations in a whisper, with a comical and amazing dislocation of the mouth,--"yes, vexing to die in the flower of one's age through the fault of a scoundrel who at this very moment is taking his coffee on the Promenade!.."

But while he thus fulminated, a clear spot began to show itself, little by little, in the sky. It snowed no more, it blew no more; and blue dashes tore away the gray of the sky. Quick, quick, ***en route***; and once more fastened to the same rope, Tartarin, who took the lead as before, turned round, put a finger on his lips, and said:--

"You know, Gonzague, that all we have just been saying is between ourselves."

"***Te! pardi***..."

Full of ardour, they started, plunging to their knees in the fresh snow, which had buried in its immaculate cotton-wool all the traces of the caravan; consequently Tartarin was forced to consult his compass every five minutes. But that Tarasconese compass, accustomed to warm climates, had been numb with cold ever since its arrival in Switzerland. The needle whirled to all four quarters, agitated, hesitating; therefore they determined to march straight before them, expecting to see the black rocks of the Grands-Mulets rise suddenly from the uniform silent whiteness of the slope, the peaks, the turrets, and ***aiguilles*** that surrounded, dazzled, and also terrified them, for who knew what dangerous crevasses it concealed beneath their feet?

"Keep cool, Gonzague, keep cool!"

"That 's just what I can't do," responded Bom-pard, in a lamentable voice. And he moaned: "***Aie***, my foot!.. ***aie***, my leg!.. we are lost; never shall we get there..."

They had walked for over two hours when, about the middle of a field of snow very difficult to climb, Bompard called out, quite terrified:--

"Tartarin, we are going ***up!***"

"Eh! ***parbleu!*** I know that well enough," returned the P. C. A., almost losing his serenity.

"But according to my ideas, we ought to be going down."

"***Be!*** yes! but how can I help it? Let's go on to the top, at any rate; it may go down on the other side."

It went down certainly--and terribly, by a succession of *neves* and glaciers, and quite at the end of this dazzling scene of dangerous whiteness a little hut was seen upon a rock at a depth which seemed to them unattainable. It was a haven that they must reach before nightfall, inasmuch as they had evidently lost the way to the Grands-Mulets, but at what cost! what efforts! what dangers, perhaps!

"Above all, don't let go of me, Gonzague, *que!*.."

"Nor you either, Tartarin."

They exchanged these requests without seeing each other, being separated by a ridge behind which Tartarin disappeared, being in advance and beginning to descend, while the other was going up, slowly and in terror. They spoke no more, concentrating all their forces, fearful of a false step, a slip. Suddenly, when Bompard was within three feet of the crest, he heard a dreadful cry from his companion, and at the same instant, the rope tightened with a violent, irregular jerk... He tried to resist, to hold fast himself and save his friend from the abyss. But the rope was old, no doubt, for it parted, suddenly, under his efforts.

"*Outre!*"

"*Boufre!*"

The two cries crossed each other, awful, heartrending, echoing through the silence and solitude, then a frightful stillness, the stillness of death that nothing more could trouble in that waste of eternal snows.

Towards evening a man who vaguely resembled Bompard, a spectre with its hair on end, muddy, soaked, arrived at the inn of the Grands-Mulets, where they rubbed him, warmed him, and put him to bed, before he could utter other words than these--choked with tears, and his hands raised to heaven: "Tartarin... lost!.. broken rope..." At last, however, they were able to make out the great misfortune which had happened.

While the old hut-man was lamenting and adding another chapter to the horrors of the mountain, hoping for fresh ossuary relics for his charnel glass-case, the Swedish youth and his guides, who had returned from their expedition, set off in search of the hapless Tartarin with ropes, ladders, in short a whole life-saving outfit, alas! unavailing... Bompard, rendered half idiotic, could give no precise indications as to the drama, nor as to the spot where it happened. They found nothing except, on the Dome du Gouter, one piece of rope which was caught in a cleft of the ice. But that piece of rope, very singular thing! was cut at both ends, as with some sharp instrument; the Chambery newspapers gave a facsimile of it, which proved the fact.

Finally, after eight days of the most conscientious search, and when the conviction became irresistible that the poor president would never be found, that he was lost beyond recall, the despairing delegates started for Tarascon, taking with them the unhappy Bompard, whose shaken brain was a visible result of the terrible shock.

"Do not talk to me about it," he replied when questioned as to the accident, "never speak to me about it again!"

Undoubtedly the White Mountain could reckon one victim the more--and what a victim!

XIV.

Epilogue.

A REGION more impressionable than Tarascon was never seen under the sun of any land. At times, of a fine festal Sunday, all the town out, tambourines a-going, the Promenade swarming, tumultuous, enamelled with red and green petticoats, Arlesian neckerchiefs, and, on big multi-coloured posters, the announcement of wrestling-matches for men and lads, races of Camargue bulls, etc., it is all-sufficient for some wag to call out: "Mad dog!" or "Cattle loose!" and everybody runs, jostles, men and women fright themselves out of their wits, doors are locked and bolted, shutters clang as with a storm, and behold Tarascon, deserted, mute, not a cat, not a sound, even the grasshoppers themselves lying low and attentive.

This was its aspect on a certain morning, which, however, was neither a fete-day nor a Sunday; the shops closed, houses dead, squares and alleys seemingly enlarged by silence and solitude. *Vasta silentio*, says Tacitus, describing Rome at the funeral of Germanicus; and that citation of his mourning Rome applies all the better to Tarascon, because a funeral service for the soul of Tartarin was being said at this moment in the cathedral, where the population *en masse* wept for its hero, its god, its invincible leader with double muscles, left lying among the glaciers of Mont Blanc.

Now, while the death-knell dropped its heavy notes along the silent streets, Mile. Tournatoire, the doctor's sister, whose ailments kept her always at home, was sitting in her big armchair close to the window, looking out into the street and listening to the bells. The house of the Tournatoires was on the road to Avignon, very nearly opposite to that of Tartarin; and the sight of that illustrious home to which its master would return no more, that garden gate forever closed, all, even the boxes of the little shoe-blacks drawn up in line near the entrance, swelled the heart of the poor spinster, consumed for more than thirty years with a secret passion for the Tarasconese hero. Oh, mystery of the heart of an old maid! It was her joy to watch him pass at his regular hours and to ask herself: "Where is he going?.." to observe the permutations of his toilet, whether he was clothed as an Alpinist or dressed in his suit of serpent-green. And now! she would see him no more! even the consolation of praying for his soul with all the other ladies of the town was denied her.

Suddenly the long white horse head of Mile. Tournatoire coloured faintly; her faded eyes with a pink rim dilated in a remarkable manner, while her thin hand with its prominent veins made the sign of the cross.. He! it *was* he, slipping along by the wall on the other side of the paved road... At first she thought it an hallucinating apparition... No, Tartarin himself, in flesh and blood, only paler, pitiable, ragged, was creeping along that wall like a beggar or a thief. But in order to explain his furtive presence in Tarascon, it is necessary to return to the Mont Blanc and the Dome du Gouter at the precise instant when, the two friends being each on either side of the ridge, Bompard felt the rope that bound them violently jerked as if by the fall of a body.

In reality, the rope was only caught in a cleft of the ice; but Tartarin, feeling the same jerk, believed, he too, that his companion was rolling down and dragging him with him. Then, at that supreme moment--good heavens! how shall I tell it?--in that agony of fear, both, at the same instant, forgetting their solemn vow at the Hotel Baltet, with the same impulse, the same instinctive action, cut the rope,--Bompard with his knife, Tartarin with his axe; then, horrified at their crime, convinced, each of them, that he had sacrificed his friend, they fled in opposite directions.

When the spectre of Bompard appeared at the Grands-Mulets, that of Tartarin was arriving at the tavern of the Avesailles. How, by what miracle? after what slips, what falls? Mont Blanc alone could tell. The poor P. C. A. remained for two days in a state of complete apathy, unable to utter a single sound. As soon as he was fit to move they took him down to Courmayeur, the Italian Chamonix. At the hotel where he stopped to recover his strength, there was talk of nothing but the frightful catastrophe on Mont Blanc, a perfect pendant to that on the Matterhorn: another Alpinist engulfed by the breaking of the rope.

In his conviction that this meant Bompard, Tartarin, torn by remorse, dared not rejoin the delegation, or return to his own town. He saw, in advance, on every lip, in every eye, the question: "Cain, what hast thou done with thy brother?.." Nevertheless, the lack of money, deficiency of linen, the frosts of September which were beginning to thin the hostelries, obliged him to set out for home. After all, no one had seen him commit the crime... Nothing hindered him from inventing some tale, no matter what... and so (the amusements of the journey lending their aid), he began to feel better. But when, on approaching Tarascon, he saw, iridescent beneath the azure heavens, the fine sky-line of the Alpines, all, all grasped him once more; shame, remorse, the fear of justice, and, to avoid the notoriety of arriving at the station, he left the train at the preceding stopping-place.

Ah! that beautiful Tarasconese highroad, all white and creaking with dust, without other shade than the telegraph poles and their wires, erected along the triumphal way he had so often trod at the head of his Alpinists and the sportsmen of caps. Would they now have known him, he, the valiant, the jauntily attired, in his ragged and filthy clothes, with that furtive eye of a tramp looking out for gendarmes? The atmosphere was burning, though the season was late, and the watermelon which he bought of a marketman seemed to him delicious as he ate it in the scanty shade of the barrow, while the peasant exhaled his wrath against the housekeepers of Tarascon, all of them absent from market that morning "on account of a black mass being sung for a man of the town who was lost in a hole, over there in the Swiss mountains... *Te!* how the bells rang... You can hear 'em from here..."

No longer any doubt. For Bompard were those lugubrious chimes of death, which a warm breeze wafted through the country solitudes.

What an accompaniment of the return of the great Tartarin to his native town!

For one moment, one, when the gate of the little garden hurriedly opened and closed behind him and Tartarin found himself at home, when he saw the little paths with their borders so neatly raked, the basin, the fountain, the gold fish (squirming as the gravel creaked beneath his feet), and the baobab giant in its mignonette pot, the comfort of that cabbage-rabbit burrow wrapped him like a security after all his dangers and adversities... But the bells, those cursed bells, tolled louder than ever; their black heavy notes fell plumb upon his heart and crushed it again. In funereal fashion they were saying to him: "Cain, what hast thou done with thy brother? Tartarin, where is Bompard?" Then, without courage to take one step, he sat down upon the hot coping of the little basin and stayed there, broken down, annihilated, to the great agitation of the gold fish.

The bells no longer toll. The porch of the cathedral, lately so resounding, is restored to the mutterings of the beggarwoman sitting by the door, and to the cold immovability of its stone saints. The religious ceremony is over; all Taras-con has gone to the Club of the Alpines, where, in solemn session, Bompard is to tell the tale of the catastrophe and relate the last moments of the P. C. A. Besides the members of the Club, many privileged persons of the army, clergy, nobility, and higher commerce have taken seats in the hall of conference, the windows of which, wide open, allow the city band, installed below on the portico, to mingle a few heroic or plaintive notes with the remarks of the gentlemen. An enormous crowd, pressing around the musicians, is standing on the tips of its toes and stretching its necks in hopes to catch a fragment of what is said in session. But the windows are too high, and no one would have any idea of what was going on without the help of two or three urchins perched in the branches of a tall linden who fling down scraps of information as they are wont to fling cherries from a tree:

"*Ve*, there's Costecalde, trying to cry. Ha! the beggar! he's got the armchair now... And that poor Bezuquet, how he blows his nose! and his eyes are all red!.. *Te!* they've put crape on the banner... There's Bompard, coming to the table with the three delegates... He has laid something down on the desk... He's speaking now... It must be fine! They are all crying..."

In truth, the grief became general as Bompard advanced in his narrative. Ah! memory had come back to him--imagination also. After picturing himself and his illustrious companion alone on the summit of Mont Blanc, without guides (who had all refused to follow them on account of the bad weather), alone with the banner, unfurled for five minutes on the highest peak of Europe, he recounted, and with what emotion! the perilous descent and fall; Tartarin rolling to the bottom of a crevasse, and he, Bompard, fastening himself to a rope two hundred feet long in order to explore that gulf to its very depths.

"More than twenty times, gentlemen--what am I saying? more than ninety times I sounded that icy abyss without being able to reach our unfortunate *presidain* whose fall, however, I was able to prove by certain fragments left clinging in the crevices of the ice..."

So saying, he spread upon the table-cloth a fragment of a tooth, some hairs from a beard, a morsel of waistcoat, and one suspender buckle; almost the whole ossuary of the Grands-Mulets.

In presence of such an exhibition the sorrowful emotions of the assembly could not be restrained; even the hardest hearts, the partisans of Costecalde, and the gravest personages--Cambalalette, the notary, the doctor, Tournatoire--shed tears as big as the stopper of a water-bottle. The invited ladies uttered heart-rending cries, smothered, however, by the sobbing howls of Excourbanies and the bleatings of Pascalon, while the funeral march of the drums and trumpets played a slow and lugubrious bass.

Then, when he saw the emotion, the nervous excitement at its height, Bompard ended his tale with a grand gesture of pity toward the scraps and the buckles, as he said:--

"And there, gentlemen and dear fellow-citizens, there is all that I recovered of our illustrious and beloved president... The remainder the glacier will restore to us in forty years..."

He was about to explain, for ignorant persons, the recent discoveries as to the slow but regular movement of glaciers, when the squeaking of a door opening at the other end of the room interrupted him; some one entered, paler than one of Home's apparitions, directly in front of the orator.

" *Ve!* Tartarin!.."

" *Te!* Gonzague!.."

And this race is so singular, so ready to believe all improbable tales, all audacious and easily refuted lies, that the arrival of the great man whose remains were still lying on the table caused only a very moderate amazement in the assembly.

"It is a misunderstanding, that's all," said Tartarin, comforted, beaming, his hand on the shoulder of the man whom he thought he had killed. "I did Mont Blanc on both sides. Went up one way and came down the other; and that is why I was thought to have disappeared."

He did not mention that he had come down on his back.

"That damned Bompard!" said Bezuquet; "all the same, he harrowed us up with his tale..." And they laughed and clasped hands, while the drums and trumpets, which they vainly tried to silence, went madly on with Tartarin's funeral march.

"*Ve!* Costecalde, just see how yellow he is!.." murmured Pascalon to Bravida, pointing to the gunsmith as he rose to yield the chair to the rightful president, whose good face beamed, Bravida, always sententious, said in a low voice as he looked at the fallen Costecalde returning to his subaltern rank: "The fate of the Abbe Mandaire, from being the rector he now is *vicaire!*"

And the session went on.

www.bookjungle.com *email: sales@bookjungle.com fax: 630-214-0564 mail: Book Jungle PO Box 2226 Champaign, IL 61825*

The Codes Of Hammurabi And Moses
W. W. Davies

QTY

The discovery of the Hammurabi Code is one of the greatest achievements of archaeology, and is of paramount interest, not only to the student of the Bible, but also to all those interested in ancient history...

Religion   **ISBN:** *1-59462-338-4*   **Pages:132**
MSRP $12.95

The Theory of Moral Sentiments
Adam Smith

QTY

This work from 1749. contains original theories of conscience amd moral judgment and it is the foundation for systemof morals.

Philosophy **ISBN:** *1-59462-777-0*   **Pages:536**
MSRP $19.95

Jessica's First Prayer
Hesba Stretton

QTY

In a screened and secluded corner of one of the many railway-bridges which span the streets of London there could be seen a few years ago, from five o'clock every morning until half past eight, a tidily set-out coffee-stall, consisting of a trestle and board, upon which stood two large tin cans, with a small fire of charcoal burning under each so as to keep the coffee boiling during the early hours of the morning when the work-people were thronging into the city on their way to their daily toil...

Pages:84

Childrens   **ISBN:** *1-59462-373-2*   **MSRP $9.95**

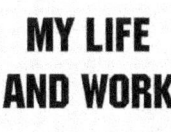

My Life and Work
Henry Ford

QTY

Henry Ford revolutionized the world with his implementation of mass production for the Model T automobile. Gain valuable business insight into his life and work with his own auto-biography... "We have only started on our development of our country we have not as yet, with all our talk of wonderful progress, done more than scratch the surface. The progress has been wonderful enough but..."

Pages:300

Biographies/   **ISBN:** *1-59462-198-5*   **MSRP $21.95**

The Art of Cross-Examination
Francis Wellman

QTY

I presume it is the experience of every author, after his first book is published upon an important subject, to be almost overwhelmed with a wealth of ideas and illustrations which could readily have been included in his book, and which to his own mind, at least, seem to make a second edition inevitable. Such certainly was the case with me; and when the first edition had reached its sixth impression in five months, I rejoiced to learn that it seemed to my publishers that the book had met with a sufficiently favorable reception to justify a second and considerably enlarged edition. ..

Pages:412

Reference   **ISBN:** *1-59462-647-2*   *MSRP $19.95*

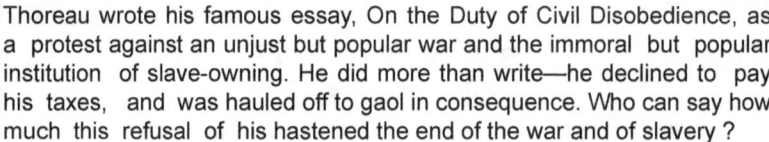

On the Duty of Civil Disobedience
Henry David Thoreau

QTY

Thoreau wrote his famous essay, On the Duty of Civil Disobedience, as a protest against an unjust but popular war and the immoral but popular institution of slave-owning. He did more than write—he declined to pay his taxes, and was hauled off to gaol in consequence. Who can say how much this refusal of his hastened the end of the war and of slavery ?

Law   **ISBN:** *1-59462-747-9*   **Pages:48**

MSRP $7.45

Dream Psychology Psychoanalysis for Beginners
Sigmund Freud

QTY

Sigmund Freud, born Sigismund Schlomo Freud (May 6, 1856 - September 23, 1939), was a Jewish-Austrian neurologist and psychiatrist who co-founded the psychoanalytic school of psychology. Freud is best known for his theories of the unconscious mind, especially involving the mechanism of repression; his redefinition of sexual desire as mobile and directed towards a wide variety of objects; and his therapeutic techniques, especially his understanding of transference in the therapeutic relationship and the presumed value of dreams as sources of insight into unconscious desires.

Pages:196

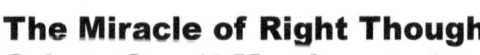

Psychology   **ISBN:** *1-59462-905-6*   *MSRP $15.45*

The Miracle of Right Thought
Orison Swett Marden

QTY

Believe with all of your heart that you will do what you were made to do. When the mind has once formed the habit of holding cheerful, happy, prosperous pictures, it will not be easy to form the opposite habit. It does not matter how improbable or how far away this realization may see, or how dark the prospects may be, if we visualize them as best we can, as vividly as possible, hold tenaciously to them and vigorously struggle to attain them, they will gradually become actualized, realized in the life. But a desire, a longing without endeavor, a yearning abandoned or held indifferently will vanish without realization.

Pages:360

Self Help   **ISBN:** *1-59462-644-8*   *MSRP $25.45*

www.bookjungle.com *email: sales@bookjungle.com fax: 630-214-0564 mail: Book Jungle PO Box 2226 Champaign, IL 61825*

QTY

The Rosicrucian Cosmo-Conception Mystic Christianity by *Max Heindel* ISBN: *1-59462-188-8* **$38.95**
The Rosicrucian Cosmo-conception is not dogmatic, neither does it appeal to any other authority than the reason of the student. It is: not controversial, but is: sent forth in the, hope that it may help to clear... New Age/Religion Pages 646

Abandonment To Divine Providence by *Jean-Pierre de Caussade* ISBN: *1-59462-228-0* **$25.95**
"The Rev. Jean Pierre de Caussade was one of the most remarkable spiritual writers of the Society of Jesus in France in the 18th Century. His death took place at Toulouse in 1751. His works have gone through many editions and have been republished... Inspirational/Religion Pages 400

Mental Chemistry by *Charles Haanel* ISBN: *1-59462-192-6* **$23.95**
Mental Chemistry allows the change of material conditions by combining and appropriately utilizing the power of the mind. Much like applied chemistry creates something new and unique out of careful combinations of chemicals the mastery of mental chemistry... New Age Pages 354

The Letters of Robert Browning and Elizabeth Barret Barrett 1845-1846 vol II ISBN: *1-59462-193-4* **$35.95**
by *Robert Browning* and *Elizabeth Barrett* Biographies Pages 596

Gleanings In Genesis (volume I) by *Arthur W. Pink* ISBN: *1-59462-130-6* **$27.45**
Appropriately has Genesis been termed "the seed plot of the Bible" for in it we have, in germ form, almost all of the great doctrines which are afterwards fully developed in the books of Scripture which follow... Religion/Inspirational Pages 420

The Master Key by *L. W. de Laurence* ISBN: *1-59462-001-6* **$30.95**
In no branch of human knowledge has there been a more lively increase of the spirit of research during the past few years than in the study of Psychology, Concentration and Mental Discipline. The requests for authentic lessons in Thought Control, Mental Discipline and... New Age/Business Pages 422

The Lesser Key Of Solomon Goetia by *L. W. de Laurence* ISBN: *1-59462-092-X* **$9.95**
This translation of the first book of the "Lernegton" which is now for the first time made accessible to students of Talismanic Magic was done, after careful collation and edition, from numerous Ancient Manuscripts in Hebrew, Latin, and French... New Age/Occult Pages 92

Rubaiyat Of Omar Khayyam by *Edward Fitzgerald* ISBN: *1-59462-332-5* **$13.95**
Edward Fitzgerald, whom the world has already learned, in spite of his own efforts to remain within the shadow of anonymity, to look upon as one of the rarest poets of the century, was born at Bredfield, in Suffolk, on the 31st of March, 1809. He was the third son of John Purcell... Music Pages 172

Ancient Law by *Henry Maine* ISBN: *1-59462-128-4* **$29.95**
The chief object of the following pages is to indicate some of the earliest ideas of mankind, as they are reflected in Ancient Law, and to point out the relation of those ideas to modern thought. Religion/History Pages 452

Far-Away Stories by *William J. Locke* ISBN: *1-59462-129-2* **$19.45**
"Good wine needs no bush, but a collection of mixed vintages does. And this book is just such a collection. Some of the stories I do not want to remain buried for ever in the museum files of dead magazine-numbers an author's not unpardonable vanity..." Fiction Pages 272

Life of David Crockett by *David Crockett* ISBN: *1-59462-250-7* **$27.45**
"Colonel David Crockett was one of the most remarkable men of the times in which he lived. Born in humble life, but gifted with a strong will, an indomitable courage, and unremitting perseverance... Biographies/New Age Pages 424

Lip-Reading by *Edward Nitchie* ISBN: *1-59462-206-X* **$25.95**
Edward B. Nitchie, founder of the New York School for the Hard of Hearing, now the Nitchie School of Lip-Reading, Inc, wrote "LIP-READING Principles and Practice". The development and perfecting of this meritorious work on lip-reading was an undertaking... How-to Pages 400

A Handbook of Suggestive Therapeutics, Applied Hypnotism, Psychic Science ISBN: *1-59462-214-0* **$24.95**
by *Henry Munro* Health/New Age/Health/Self-help Pages 376

A Doll's House: and Two Other Plays by *Henrik Ibsen* ISBN: *1-59462-112-8* **$19.95**
Henrik Ibsen created this classic when in revolutionary 1848 Rome. Introducing some striking concepts in playwriting for the realist genre, this play has been studied the world over. Fiction/Classics/Plays 308

The Light of Asia by *sir Edwin Arnold* ISBN: *1-59462-204-3* **$13.95**
In this poetic masterpiece, Edwin Arnold describes the life and teachings of Buddha. The man who was to become known as Buddha to the world was born as Prince Gautama of India but he rejected the worldly riches and abandoned the reigns of power when... Religion/History/Biographies Pages 170

The Complete Works of Guy de Maupassant by *Guy de Maupassant* ISBN: *1-59462-157-8* **$16.95**
"For days and days, nights and nights, I had dreamed of that first kiss which was to consecrate our engagement, and I knew not on what spot I should put my lips..." Fiction/Classics Pages 240

The Art of Cross-Examination by *Francis L. Wellman* ISBN: *1-59462-309-0* **$26.95**
Written by a renowned trial lawyer, Wellman imparts his experience and uses case studies to explain how to use psychology to extract desired information through questioning. How-to/Science/Reference Pages 408

Answered or Unanswered? by *Louisa Vaughan* ISBN: *1-59462-248-5* **$10.95**
Miracles of Faith in China Religion Pages 112

The Edinburgh Lectures on Mental Science (1909) by *Thomas* ISBN: *1-59462-008-3* **$11.95**
This book contains the substance of a course of lectures recently given by the writer in the Queen Street Hall, Edinburgh. Its purpose is to indicate the Natural Principles governing the relation between Mental Action and Material Conditions... New Age/Psychology Pages 148

Ayesha by *H. Rider Haggard* ISBN: *1-59462-301-5* **$24.95**
Verily and indeed it is the unexpected that happens! Probably if there was one person upon the earth from whom the Editor of this, and of a certain previous history, did not expect to hear again... Classics Pages 380

Ayala's Angel by *Anthony Trollope* ISBN: *1-59462-352-X* **$29.95**
The two girls were both pretty, but Lucy who was twenty-one who supposed to be simple and comparatively unattractive, whereas Ayala was credited, as her Bombwhat romantic name might show, with poetic charm and a taste for romance. Ayala when her father died was nineteen... Fiction Pages 484

The American Commonwealth by *James Bryce* ISBN: *1-59462-286-8* **$34.45**
An interpretation of American democratic political theory. It examines political mechanics and society from the perspective of Scotsman James Bryce Politics Pages 572

Stories of the Pilgrims by *Margaret P. Pumphrey* ISBN: *1-59462-116-0* **$17.95**
This book explores pilgrims religious oppression in England as well as their escape to Holland and eventual crossing to America on the Mayflower, and their early days in New England... History Pages 268

QTY

The Fasting Cure *by Sinclair Upton*　　ISBN: *1-59462-222-1*　**$13.95**
In the Cosmopolitan Magazine for May, 1910, and in the Contemporary Review (London) for April, 1910, I published an article dealing with my experiences in fasting. I have written a great many magazine articles, but never one which attracted so much attention... New Age/Self Help/Health Pages 164

Hebrew Astrology *by Sepharial*　　ISBN: *1-59462-308-2*　**$13.45**
In these days of advanced thinking it is a matter of common observation that we have left many of the old landmarks behind and that we are now pressing forward to greater heights and to a wider horizon than that which represented the mind-content of our progenitors... Astrology Pages 144

Thought Vibration or The Law of Attraction in the Thought World　　ISBN: *1-59462-127-6*　**$12.95**
by William Walker Atkinson　　Psychology/Religion Pages 144

Optimism *by Helen Keller*　　ISBN: *1-59462-108-X*　**$15.95**
Helen Keller was blind, deaf, and mute since 19 months old, yet famously learned how to overcome these handicaps, communicate with the world, and spread her lectures promoting optimism. An inspiring read for everyone... Biographies/Inspirational Pages 84

Sara Crewe *by Frances Burnett*　　ISBN: *1-59462-360-0*　**$9.45**
In the first place, Miss Minchin lived in London. Her home was a large, dull, tall one, in a large, dull square, where all the houses were alike, and all the sparrows were alike, and where all the door-knockers made the same heavy sound... Childrens/Classic Pages 88

The Autobiography of Benjamin Franklin *by Benjamin Franklin*　　ISBN: *1-59462-135-7*　**$24.95**
The Autobiography of Benjamin Franklin has probably been more extensively read than any other American historical work, and no other book of its kind has had such ups and downs of fortune. Franklin lived for many years in England, where he was agent... Biographies/History Pages 332

Name	
Email	
Telephone	
Address	
City, State ZIP	

☐ **Credit Card**　　　☐ **Check / Money Order**

Credit Card Number	
Expiration Date	
Signature	

Please Mail to:　Book Jungle
PO Box 2226
Champaign, IL 61825
or Fax to:　　　630-214-0564

ORDERING INFORMATION

web*: www.bookjungle.com*
email*: sales@bookjungle.com*
fax*: 630-214-0564*
mail*: Book Jungle PO Box 2226 Champaign, IL 61825*
or PayPal *to sales@bookjungle.com*

Please contact us for bulk discounts

DIRECT-ORDER TERMS

**20% Discount if You Order
Two or More Books**
Free Domestic Shipping!
Accepted: Master Card, Visa,
Discover, American Express